Dope-Darling

Dope-Darling

A Story of Cocaine

David Garnett

MINT EDITIONS

Dope-Darling: A Story of Cocaine was first published in 1919.

This edition published by Mint Editions 2021.

ISBN 9781513212227 | E-ISBN 9781513212210

Published by Mint Editions®

MINT
EDITIONS

minteditionbooks.com

Publishing Director: Jennifer Newens
Design & Production: Rachel Lopez Metzger
Project Manager: Micaela Clark
Typesetting: Westchester Publishing Services

Contents

I

"Will you marry me?" When Roy Gordon asked Beatrice Chase this question he was kneeling before her in a corn-field, where she sat on a pile of sheaves picking fragments of golden chaff from out the raven blackness of his hair.

She sat silent through a moment of happiness that was almost anguish; her fingers, still touching his curly head, trembled and closed mechanically. Looking down, she found his blue eyes fixed on her. Beatrice's heart was too full for words; she could only smile and nod her acceptance. It seemed to her that she had never seen Roy looking so handsome. His shirt was open at the neck, his sleeves rolled up and his face red with working in the sun.

At that moment Roy was thinking the same about Beatrice; he had never seen her so calm, so beautiful.

At last Beatrice could find her voice and asked:

"But are you sure you want me to?"

"I shouldn't ask you if I didn't," said Roy, and taking her hand in his he covered it with kisses. It was some time before he spoke again, to say: "Darling, then we are engaged to be married." And plucking a straw out of the sheaf he began winding it round her finger. It made, when it was done, a band of pale gold.

"Please regard this as an engagement ring—until we get a better one," he said, smiling.

"How simple it seems to do what one wants to, when one has done it."

Beatrice leant forward and kissed him. She knew what Roy meant. They had known each other all their lives, and there had never been any sentiment or lovers' talk between them. Yet they loved each other, only something had made it hard to speak, something that made the words of love seem unreal.

For a long time they sat there looking into each other's eyes. It was the close of a perfect day, the second of Beatrice's holiday after her final examination as a doctor, which she had pased with flying colours. They had risen early in the great house in the north of Scotland where they were staying with Roy's cousins, and had gone for a ride together before breakfast. They had galloped up to the bare side of the moor where there was nothing but short heather and ling, and the mist still lay like white pools in the corries. Startled deer had sprung up half-a-mile away, and vanished as suddenly. Afterwards they had made their way slowly down the steep hillside through a forest of dark Scotch firs.

Their horses stumbled, and wood-pigeons rose with a great clatter of wings. After breakfast, Roy had seen the harvesters working, and had gone to help them on the spur of the moment. Beatrice had worked with him, tying sheaves, in the morning, but in the afternoon she had brought a book and sat looking on. She had felt happy as she had not done since she was a little girl in short frocks.

As their houses were next door to each other, Roy and Beatrice had always been like brother and sister. In those days of childhood Beatrice had been perfectly happy till Roy had been sent off to school at Rugby and afterwards to Cambridge, while she had gone to a boarding school and, like Roy, had afterwards become a medical student.

They walked back across the stubble in the last rays of the setting sun with their arms round each other. From the edge of the upland field they looked down on the rushing torrent that swept past a hundred feet below them and dashed itself from rock to rock in cascades of foam.

Beatrice suddenly felt Roy's hand relax; he stood as if petrified, and she saw that he was looking at something. He seemed to have forgotten her existence, for when she spoke to him he started visibly and frowned before he spoke.

"The osprey!" he exclaimed, but did not point, and Beatrice began to feel annoyed with him.

"Where?" she asked; but at that moment the osprey rose from a tree below them, and mounting quickly on immense grey pointed wings flew rapidly towards the distant lake. Roy gazed after it spell-bound.

Beatrice felt suddenly unreasonably depressed. It seemed to her that what she had often felt before was still true, and that even if he did not think so, she was not the right person for Roy. She felt that though Roy loved her she did not charm him, or amuse him. She felt she was too dull, too heavy. When Roy spoke, his words added to her depression.

"I shall never, never forget seeing that bird. I would rather have missed anything than that."

Something was wrong, yet Beatrice was in love with Roy herself. She knew Roy through and through, and believed he was her superior in everything that really mattered. She worshipped him blindly, as a woman does; but it was difficult to say she was not right. Roy Gordon had everything to make him loved by the women and envied by the men. Young, handsome, generous, he had no fault or flaw that could be detected. Indeed, his only fault was that he was too sensitive to other people's feelings to care first and foremost about getting his own way. He was plucky enough if he were the person to suffer, but he could not bear to hurt other people. But this failure to push himself was only the reverse side of his good qualities, and, moreover, like his complete lack of fear, it was in his blood. The Gordons had never pushed themselves, because they had never needed to push themselves. Roy came of a noble house, and in an age when reckless courage was all that had been required of a gentleman, its sons had been the fairest amid the flowers of the Scotch nobility.

Nobody was surprised when Roy and Beatrice became engaged; they were such old friends that many people thought they had been engaged for years. And certainly nobody would have taken them for a newly engaged couple. The role of lovers sat ill upon them, though each had hidden fires and depths of passions that they did not guess at themselves.

For Beatrice the thought that she was to marry Roy was a deep source of happiness, but she did not dwell on it. Meantime there were examinations Roy had to pass, so she talked shop. They were to be married after he had qualified—in a year's time.

II

When Roy came into her sitting-room at St. Xavier's Hospital two days before his final examination, expecting a hard evening's grind in preparation for it, Beatrice greeted him with a quick smile, and rather to his surprise kissed him.

"We mustn't overdo it," she said, "you'll pass easily now, I feel sure; if we go on you'll get stale. Give me a kiss, and take me to the theatre."

Roy did as he was told, and in the brilliant restaurant where they dined, listening to the strains of a hidden band playing ragtime, Roy realised that he was staler than he had thought.

"I've never worked so hard before in my life," he said; "if I don't pass now I never shall."

Beatrice laughed. "I don't suppose you ever have worked harder, or will ever have to work as hard again. I hope not. Now no more shop."

"Do you realise I haven't dined out for ever so long, not for months?"

She nodded. She did realise it, and she knew that it was her doing that he had taken his work so seriously, and that when he passed brilliantly it would be a great deal due to her. If he passed this examination, as she felt sure he would, he would have taken the shortest time possible in which to qualify as a doctor. He had done brilliantly in the last year, and she had heard him spoken of as one of the most promising students that had ever been known in his hospital.

"What's that tune?" Roy asked, as the band stopped playing. "That's new." He whistled it over, and, as Beatrice did not know, Roy beckoned a waiter and sent him to find out.

"What? 'It's a Long Way to Tipperary'! I never heard of it," he said when the man returned with the required information. Roy was to hear it more often than he thought, in strange places and with strange companions.

From the restaurant they went to the "Passing Show," a new revue at the Palace, with Gaby Deslys and Basil Hallam. Beatrice felt perfectly happy as they sat there through the first part of the performance. She was in high spirits. Roy, too, was contented, though he was rather absent-minded and unresponsive as he so often was when he was alone with Beatrice.

DAVID GARNETT

During the interval a friendly hand touched him on the shoulder, and a friendly voice said:

"What, Roy here! How wonderful to see you, and Beatrice too; so you've got your keeper! Is the exam over? How've you done? What? Oh, not till the day after tomorrow? Do you know Molly Withers? Oh, of course you do."

It was Robert Brewer, a journalist whom they both knew slightly. Brewer was always gay, always happy, always glad to see people, always talking, and naturally enough everyone was always glad to see him. He was with a girl from the Slade School of Art, whom Beatrice had met once or twice at country houses and at London parties, and as Molly always had something amusing to say, she had taken rather a fancy to her.

After the performance Brewer insisted on taking them on to a night club which he had just joined.

"You must come on to my club; really for anybody working in Fleet Street it's essential to have a club you can go to at any time in the early hours."

Beatrice looked at her watch.

"Yes—it won't do you any harm, Roy," she decided, "but you must be in bed by twelve." The phrase about being Roy's keeper rankled, and she meant to show it was not altogether justified.

They found the club only a few doors off, and after Brewer had put their names down in the visitor's book, they went upstairs.

As they entered a big dirty room at the top of the house, they heard a woman singing, and stood silent in the doorway. The room was full of tables at one end, where perhaps fifty people were sitting and drinking; there was a bar at the side of the room. The air was thick with tobacco smoke, and everything was dirty, shoddy and meretricious; it was not even comfortable!

But Roy was only aware for one moment of the sordidess of his surroundings; all his attention was taken up with the girl who was singing. She was small and slim, and most extraordinarily lovely, but dressed very simply. She had that wonderful beauty that is found only in England, and in the country.

She was fresh as a rosebud still touched by the morning dew.

It was difficult to imagine indeed how she had got to such a place for she did not look more than seventeen. To add to his enchantment the song she was singing was so fresh, such a relief after all the nigger melodies and syncopation that then held London in their grip, that Roy could hardly believe his ears.

"Who is Silvia? what is she?"

The girl sang Shakespeare's words with the simplicity and innocence of a milkmaid straying along a country lane and gathering a nosegay of wild briar by the way. Her voice was not powerful, but the very amateurishness of the performance constituted part of its charm.

Roy felt like a man bewitched. He felt he had never before seen or heard anything so beautiful in his life.

After his years of monotonous study, living, as he had once complained to Beatrice, in a septic nightmare, the scales seemed to drop from his eyes.

Why should he waste his youth amid scenes of suffering and ugliness, sufferings which, when all was said and done, he could do so little to relieve?

When she had finished her song amid considerable applause, Roy found that the girl had turned round and was looking at him in the doorway.

She came towards them with a rosy blush and said:

"Thank you all so much for not interrupting me. Please come in."

"Hullo, Claire!" said Brewer.

She shook hands with him, but her eyes were fixed for a moment on Roy with a queer look that thrilled him through and through.

What was happening to him? Everything except those starry eyes became remote and dim. Brewer found them a table and ordered drinks. When Beatrice suggested chocolate Roy agreed vaguely.

After a few minutes a string band assembled and began playing a lively dance tune. Roy was passionately fond of dancing, and jumped up at once and turned to Beatrice. He was glad of an opportunity to shake off his queer mood. When she refused he stood for a moment irresolutely.

"Go and dance," said Beatrice, "if you want to."

She was peeling an apple, and pretending it was a surgical operation.

Roy still paused and looked up at the other dancers beginning the Tango. A moment afterwards he started forward; he had met Claire's eye, and she had beckoned to him. He was lost in a stupor and danced madly, blindly, forgetting where he was, or what was happening to him.

She was a splendid partner, and they danced wonderfully, in silence, with an almost religious intensity.

His skill, and the reckless abandon which Claire threw into her movements attracted the attention of the company, some of whom drew near to watch them.

They were the centre of interest, and when the music stopped with a crash they were greeted with loud applause and cries of "Bravo!"

Roy thanked Claire conventionally, and went back to where the others were sitting.

Beatrice greeted him with "Well done! Aren't you glad now you didn't dance with me?" She looked at her watch and rose from the table. "It's time we were off."

Roy followed her mechanically. What, what had happened to him?

They found a taxi, and Beatrice dropped him with some parting words at his flat, on her way to St. Xavier's Hospital.

"Now sleep well, there's a good boy," she said, "and don't get up too early in the morning. If you call in about five I shall be free, and we'll run over those last few points."

Roy found he was being kissed. The taxi drove off and he let himself in at his door.

Roy went up to his rooms, but for some hours he did not think of going to bed, but sat with his head in his hands, staring at a blank patch of wall, while the gas hissed and spluttered.

III

Beatrice looked again at her watch.

It was five minutes to six. She was tired of waiting and hungry. Taking the kettle off the fire she made tea and fetched a buttered muffin off a pile that had been keeping warm in the grate for an hour. What could be the matter? Before she had drunk half the cup, she jumped up with a worried look on her face, and began walking up and down the room.

Why didn't Roy come?

After half an hour more Beatrice wrote a note: "Shall be back at seven," and leaving it on the table for Roy, went out, meaning to go round to his flat to try and find him. Perhaps he had caught a cold, or had forgotten.

As she was going out, she glanced up at the letter rack. There was a note for her in Roy's handwriting! It ran:

> Dear Beatrice,
>   I shan't come in this evening as I am not at all in the
> mood for work. I promise you I shall pass the examination.
>
> Roy

Beatrice laughed, and went back to her room feeling very foolish. But why on earth if Roy had left the note, hadn't he come up?

On second thoughts she was not so reassured. What could be the matter with Roy, she wondered; he had seemed queer last night: Beatrice remembered the dance. She had not seen him like that since she had gone to Cambridge in May week and he was in the winning boat in the bump races.

Yes, Beatrice felt worried; but later on she changed her clothes and rang up Brewer. He would be able to distract her. They met in a crowded cafe, and by the time dinner was over she had regained her spirits.

They sat and talked for some time over their coffee and cigarettes, then Brewer suggested going again to his club.

Ordinarily Beatrice would not have cared to do so, but suddenly an idea flashed into her mind that made her accept, almost eagerly.

It was not far, so they walked.

While Brewer was putting their names down Beatrice looked over his shoulder. To her horror her worst fears were justified. Roy had signed his name just above where Brewer was now writing hers!

Whom was he the guest of?

Beatrice looked again and saw the name "Claire" written in an ungainly hand. The next moment Robert Brewer had turned round with a self-conscious laugh.

"I say, Beatrice," he began, "I know you'll think me a most unutterable ass; but do you mind if we don't go up? There's someone here whom I simply can't bear to meet. It's a woman; and the fact of the matter is I proposed to her two days ago and she turned me down."

Yes, Robert was lying, Beatrice felt sure of that; but she liked him the better for it; she turned to go as she said:

"No, don't let's go up. I don't want to a bit."

"I'll tell you about it," said the versatile Brewer, pushing the book away.

"No, please don't," said Beatrice. "Not unless you want to, that is."

Brewer motioned to the doorkeeper, who opened the door for them. It had come on to rain slightly, so Brewer whistled for a taxi. While they were waiting Beatrice saw two people coming out after them, and in the light of the open door she saw it was Roy and Claire. A taxi drove up, but the next moment Brewer seized her arm and was leading her away down the street.

"That was her," said Brewer. "Please excuse my behaviour. Please. . ."

But Beatrice was not listening to him. The next moment she heard Roy's voice giving the cabman the address of his own flat.

Roy was taking that woman home with him!

Brewer took her to an Appenrodts, and Beatrice found herself wondering why she had come. She hardly could believe it of Roy. It was awful! Awful! And it was typical of Beatrice that her first feeling was not jealousy. She was not jealous; she was worried. She was worried on Roy's account, at his playing the fool like this the night before his examination, at his throwing away months of work. It was dreadful. She could not believe it of him. Beatrice thought of his note with its absurd "I promise you I shall pass the exam." What did that mean?

Oh, it was too much! She couldn't stand it any longer. She found Brewer was staring at her. He had been telling her something and she wasn't attending.

"I'm sorry, Bob, I'm rather off colour tonight and worried about Roy. I think if you'll get me a taxi I'll go home."

Brewer was upset, he saw his manœuvre had been in vain.

"I'm so sorry I took you to that beastly club," he cried. "Cheer up, Beatrice. Roy's certain to do well tomorrow."

He shook hands at parting, and his warm grip was meant to be comforting.

"What a good fellow Brewer is," she thought to herself in the taxi, then sinking back she murmured: "Oh, Roy, Roy, whatever do you mean by being such a fool? Can't you see! Can't you see! But perhaps it was all right, and she was only being absurdly suspicious and jealous for no reason. For a long time after she got back Beatrice couldn't get to sleep. Then she said to herself: "After all its only an exam. If he fails now, he'll go in again next year and I'll be sure he gets through then." With that resolution she fell asleep.

IV

All that day Roy Gordon had not been able to look at his books or his slides. He had planned to look through a collection of microscope slides, but when he sat down he found his fingers were trembling and he couldn't focus the instrument. He jumped up in a rage, and walked up and down the room excitedly.

When he thought of Beatrice, he groaned. What a ghastly position it was! He was in honour bound to Beatrice, but he was madly in love with the girl he had danced with—Claire. He knew now that he had never before known what love was. He forced himself to sit down with a book, but after a few moments reading, found he could not understand what he had just read, or remember what it was about. It was impossible to do any work.

I must see her again, he thought to himself. Perhaps when I see her it will all be quite different. I must see her again, and then I'll tell Beatrice, and if in six months time I still feel like this. . . Probably Claire wouldn't look at him, but it was clear to him that if it was dishonourable to break off his engagement with Beatrice, it was still more dishonourable to marry her while he was feeling like this about another woman.

Supposing he had not met Claire until after he and Beatrice were married! How awful it would have been! He had known Beatrice such a long time, he reflected, with an inward groan. That was the horrible part of it. Poor, poor Beatrice. Roy could not conceal from himself the fact that Beatrice really cared for him, was in love with him.

Oh, I wish I could make myself be in love with her! But he saw that he wasn't, that he never had been, and that probably he never would be in love with Beatrice.

"What a blackguard I am," he murmured to himself. That day was an agony for Roy. He sat thinking it all over in his room, and two things at least stood out plain to him. He must tell Beatrice, and he must pass the examination. If he failed in that, he would wound Beatrice even more than he would injure himself. It would be ignominious to fail.

At a quarter to five he hurried round to St. Xavier's Hospital. In the entrance, he suddenly realised that he could not face Beatrice like that. It would upset her too much to see him in such a state. Roy wrote a note for Beatrice, and put it in the rack. After he had gone out, he thought to himself:

"I'll tell her after the exam, and then, at least, she'll have the consolation of knowing I've passed it." But no sooner had this entered Roy's head than he saw it was a cruel and ignoble thought.

"I must be honest; I must tell Beatrice now, at once. I cannot see her and behave as if nothing had happened. I cannot keep her waiting in suspense for three days. The least I can do is to be quite honest." Saying this to himself, Roy went into a post office and wrote a letter to Beatrice, which he sealed, stamped, and posted. He had had no food all day, but it did not occur to him that he was hungry as he walked slowly up and down the embankment by the river. Later on in the evening, it occurred to him that if he could find Brewer he would be able to find out who Claire was. Brewer knew Claire. With this object, he went to the night club in Soho, and rang the bell.

The door was opened, and in the hall he saw Claire turning over the pages of the visitors' book.

"Is Mr. Brewer here?" he asked the porter.

"No, sir. Mr. Brewer hasn't been in tonight, sir."

"Can I go up and wait for him?" asked Roy.

"I'm very sorry, sir, but it's quite impossible; the Club rules is. . ."

"Oh. . ." said a shy voice. "Won't you be my guest, Mr. Gordon?" It was Claire speaking.

Roy thanked her, and wrote his name down opposite hers.

"I've been asking everybody about you," said Claire, giving him a singular look. "None of them knew, and I have only just found out that your name is Roy Gordon. I was looking for it in the book. Do you know mine? It's Plowman, Claire Plowman. Everybody calls me Claire."

A few moments later, she said: "Will you have dinner with me? I'm all alone. We can have it sent in here, you know."

Roy said that he would be charmed. He was in a dreamy state; he could hardly believe in what was happening to him, yet everything was clear and definite in his mind. He would not speak yet. Claire told him, in that queer shy way she had, things that no girl Roy had ever met would have said.

"I've been thinking about you ever since I saw you. I sat up all last night thinking about you."

Roy might have said that he had done the same, but refrained. Claire's words set him on fire: he had never met a woman who had told him so clearly that he had made an impression. Perhaps he would not have liked it if the extraordinary boldness of Claire's words had not been contradicted by the shyness and soft confusion with which she uttered them. Claire was at once delicate and vigorous, and could combine at the same moment the shyness and the intrepid boldness of a child.

She ordered dinner: oysters, grilled steak, curried prawns, a bottle of champagne, and two Zabaglionis—Zabaglionis are the yolks of eggs beaten up in Marsala, a dish of which Claire was extremely fond.

After his long fast, Roy ate and drank freely. His gloomy heart-searchings disappeared, and after two glasses of champagne he felt perfectly happy.

Claire sat in front of him on the other side of the table, and as he gazed into her starry eyes Roy knew that nothing else existed for him in the world, and that he would stoop to any baseness and commit any villainy to win her love.

Claire ordered coffee, brandy, and cigarettes, and began telling him her story. As Roy heard it, the colour slowly left his face, and, with his fists clenched, he sat silent.

"My father was a carrier at Fairford, in Gloucester. My mother was a showman's daughter. She ran away soon after I was born. When I was twelve years old, I saw an old gentleman having a fit. He was lying on his face in the middle of the road, with his head in a puddle of water, so I pulled him out, turned him over, and fetched the doctor. He adopted me, and sent me to a good school. Four years ago I ran away, and came to London. I didn't know anyone, and wandered about near Paddington Station. When I had spent all my money, I went and sat in Hyde Park. While I was sitting there, an old gentleman came up and made faces at me, and asked me if I was hungry. I said 'Yes.' So he took me to an A.B.C. in Notting Hill Gate, and told me to be a good girl and say my prayers. After he left me, a young man came up and asked me if I wanted plenty of money and little to do. He took me to Shepherds Bush to a house, and gave me something funny to drink. I went off to sleep, and when I woke up there was a black man in the room with me. After that, several others came. I got out of the window and dropped into the area, and ran away. I slept that night in Hyde Park. Next morning a park-keeper found me, and took me home with him. He and his wife were very good to me, and kept me for a fortnight. Then a girl spoke to me in Regent Street, and took me as her maid. One of her friends was an actor. He asked me to sing, and then said he'd get me a job on the Brighton Pier. I got thirty shillings a week there. Three months ago, the old gentleman who adopted me in Fairford died, and left me all his money. That's my story. What's yours?"

Before Roy had time to answer, a man came up and asked Claire if she would sing.

"No! no! no!" she cried, passionately. "Go away."

Roy eyed the man angrily. The stranger was apparently going to make some remark, but thought better of it, and withdrew.

"Take me somewhere where we can talk in peace," said Claire. "This place is getting too full—and it's a beastly place anyhow."

"Come back to my flat."

"All right." Claire looked at him very straight right in the eyes, and added, "Can you put me up for the night?"

Roy nodded; he could not trust his voice. Claire beckoned to the waiter, and gave him three or four pounds in gold. Roy intervened.

"Nonsense," said Claire. "I'm a member here, you're not." Then, as he helped her on with her Chinese cloak of heavy silk: "I don't like being paid for by men. I'm not a prostitute, though I've been pretty near it."

Roy had nothing to say. They walked out, and got into a taxi that had just driven up.

"How old are you?" asked Roy, in the cab.

"Eighteen."

Then, as they turned into Shaftsbury Avenue, Claire leant out of the window, and asked the driver to stop. Roy watched her disappear into a chemist's. She came back, laughing merrily.

"Were you afraid I had run away?" she asked him.

"No," said Roy. "I hadn't thought of that."

"Good. I wanted some cocaine, that's all. I take it."

"You shouldn't," said Roy. He was overwhelmed by all that was happening; by all that he heard; he wanted time to think. How could such horrors be combined with so much beauty?

He could see her eyes staring at him in the dark, but they said nothing more till they reached his flat. Once there, Roy lit the fire, then brought chairs.

Claire was standing at the other end of the room looking at his things.

"Well?" she said.

"Well. I'm twenty-five. My father was a colonel, and was killed in the Boer War."

"Don't tell me all that," said Claire. "Everybody's story is the same, really." But she looked at him, and her eyes blazed. Then she opened a little box, and began sniffing a white powder up her nose.

"Don't do that. Don't do that," cried Roy. He sprang forward, and caught her by the writst.

"Why not?" Claire was serious, and prepared to be resentful.

"Because I'm in love with you, because you'll kill yourself if you take that beastly stuff."

Claire took a deep breath; her eyes sparkled like diamonds.

"I love you; I'm in love with you," said Roy. Then he added: "Will you marry me?"

Claire shook her head.

"No, I should ruin you. Marry that girl you were with last night."

"That can never happen now. I wrote to her this evening, and told her I was in love with you. I asked her to break off our engagement."

Claire wondered. Doubt opened in her mind, and separated them. Roy was standing close to her, still holding her by one hand. He drew Claire towards him and kissed her, but as he did so Claire jumped, jumped as if she had accidentally touched hot iron.

"Let me go—why did you bring me here? Do you think I am a prostitute, or do you want money?"

Roy stepped back, and stared at her haughtily. He could scarcely believe his senses, as Claire went on:

"You think, because you have got me here alone, you can do as you like. You're a brute."

Claire shrank away from him like a frightened animal. She put her hands behind her flat against the wall. Roy was angry.

"I think I had better show you your room, if you mean to stay."

"You want to turn me out because you've failed to seduce me, I suppose," said Claire.

She followed Roy into the next room, where he lit the gas, and left without saying good-night. He undressed rapidly, and made up a bed for himself on the sofa; when he lay down his heart was beating violently. "Cocaine," he said to himself. "Oh, my God, how awful it is!"

A little while afterwards the door opened softly, and Claire came in dressed loosely in a pair of his silk pyjamas, which she must have found in his drawer. She came in and, without noticing him, sat down in front of the fire. In the firelight he could see her fleece of golden hair, and the soft curve of her back showing through the silk. She was warming her hands.

For a long time Roy would not move or speak. At last he said, quietly:

"Do you mind going to your room and letting me go to sleep? My final examination is tomorrow."

Claire looked round.

"I didn't know you were there. I came in to warm myself at the fire. I'm as cold as ice."

"There's a gas fire in your room," said Roy. He sat up on the edge of the sofa. Claire lost her temper.

"You're a cold-blooded bully; you look like a stuffed fish in the parlour. I'm not going to be ordered about by you. I'll teach you a lesson, just because you are a coward. What you said was all lies. You're not in the least in love with me; you don't want to marry me. You haven't got an examination. You thought you would seduce me easily by telling lies: you might have had a chance if you had been honest. When you saw it wasn't so easy, you put me to sleep in a frozen room." After a moment, she added, with contempt: "I shall do just as I like. I'm master here."

Roy jumped up, and pointed at the door, then he said:

"Well, if you won't go, I shall turn you out." He strode over, and caught her by the wrists.

Claire spat in his face. At that, something boiled up in Roy that he had never known was there. He caught at Claire, picked her right off the ground, and carried her towards the door.

Claire dug her nails into his flesh and bit at him, and Roy found himself shaking her violently as a terrier shakes a rat.

Claire let go, and suddenly whispered to him, "Darling, darling, I love you," and Roy was almost strangled with the frenzy of her embraces. "Darling, darling!"

ROY WOKE EARLY, AND FOUND Claire sleeping in his arms. Such beauty he had never seen before. He held his breath, as if she were some rare butterfly that would be frightened away by any movement. Ten minutes afterwards, she opened her eyes, and smiled seraphically.

In those ten minutes Roy had made up his mind; he had burnt his boats. He would marry Claire, and cure her of taking drugs. Nothing on earth could come between him and Claire. He saw what fate might have in store for him: he defied fate, he defied death, he defied cocaine.

"Will you marry me?" he asked her directly she woke up.

Claire was surprised. "Do you mean really?"

"Of course."

"Yes. . . I think so. I shall ruin you. You don't know what I am." She spoke sadly; tears came into her eyes. Roy kissed her. Later on, he said:

"You'll give up taking cocaine. I'll help you do that. I'm a doctor."

"Yes, I promise. I'll never take it again, I promise. I promise," Claire repeated, passionately.

They were silent for a while. Then:

"You must get up, darling, if it's true about your examination."

Roy laughed. He had never felt so happy as on that morning while Claire and he sat eating grapefruit for breakfast.

It was a lovely morning; the sunshine came streaming into the room.

"I've never been in love before in my life," said Claire. "I fell in love with you at first sight. You are really in love with me, aren't you? It is all real?"

Roy took her in his arms.

"Will you ever forgive me," she went on, "for last night?"

"Silly creature."

"I shan't come near you again till you've done your exam," she said next. "And I won't touch cocaine."

"Meet me the day after tomorrow, at six o'clock."

Roy and Claire parted in the street outside the Royal College of Surgeons. Claire stood watching him with tender eyes until he had vanished into the building.

V

T he evening after the examination, Beatrice Chase sat alone in her room in St. Xaxier's Hospital thinking. . .

She had heard nothing from Roy. She had had nothing but a postcard, saying, "Can I please come and see you tomorrow morning before lunch?—Roy."

What could it mean? Beatrice had to go on duty in the out-patient ward that night. She slipped on a long white linen coat, and rose wearily. Was all her labour to have been in vain? Her love to be wasted inexplicably? What was the matter? How could Roy behave so to her? Her lips hardened.

She worked wearily, almost mechanically, attending to the people who had accidents in the streets, tying up cut fingers, looking at drunk women. There was a man who had tried to drown himself in one of the fountains in Trafalgar Square, and naturally had not succeeded, a scalded baby, a boy with a crushed foot.

At two o'clock in the morning there was a ring at the gate, and two policemen came in with a man on a stretcher.

"Good evening, doctor. . . We picked this fellow up like this in Francis Street at one thirty-five." They laid the stretcher on a bare bed. Beatrice nodded. She was used to the police bringing in all sorts of people; they were mostly drunk. She unhooked her stethoscope, and was actually stooping over the body when she recognised that it was Roy.

For a moment her nerve failed her, and she stood leaning over him with her head swimming, afraid to trust her voice, afraid she would faint.

Then she recovered herself, and with a great effort of self-control smelt Roy's breath. He smelt of spirits, but not strongly. Beatrice undid his waistcoat and unbuttoned his shirt, inwardly marvelling at her steady fingers. She listened to his heart. It was beating steadily.

Beatrice raised her head, and gave the foremost policeman a charming smile.

"You don't want him, do you, sergeant?"

"Lor' bless you, miss, we don't want him if you don't mind keeping him."

"All right—the poor fellow's had some kind of a seizure."

"That's just what I thought myself, doctor," said the policeman, with a grin. "Shall we leave him on the bed here?"

"No—" said Beatrice, "do you mind bringing him into this little room?"

They carried Roy into a separate room, and rolled him off on to the bed.

Roy scarcely stirred. He lay there limply. A few minutes later Beatrice came in and began a detailed examination of him. She reluctantly had to come to the conclusion that there was nothing much the matter. Roy was drunk.

This was the last straw, and anger flamed up in Beatrice's grey eyes, as she stood back and gazed at Roy.

He lay peacefully as if he were asleep, looking handsome and dignified with his fastidious mouth closed, and his black hair rather ruffled. His face was very pale, and indeed at that moment Roy looked more like a young crusader sleeping by the camp-fire than a drunken sot who had been picked up blind to the world in a London street.

But Beatrice judged him as he lay there, and found him wanting. He was a coward, a shirker, and a drunkard. Roy had muffed his exam, had funked it, and had tried to forget his failure by getting drunk. Then there was that woman!

Beatrice could not even feel sure that Roy had turned up at the examination: for some reason his nerve had suddenly failed him, and she felt that Roy was utterly contemptible. He knew his subject fairly well, he had worked hard for months, and then he had funked it at the last minute. . . Roy a coward! Oh, it was too much!

Beatrice went off duty at four o'clock in the morning, leaving instructions that she was to be sent for if he showed any signs of returning consciousness. She was very tired, yet it was a long time before she could get to sleep.

VI

When Beatrice woke up, it was broad daylight, and the clock of the church near by was striking twelve.

What had happened to Roy, she wondered, and, dressing hastily, went into her sitting-room.

She found that her breakfast had been brought up, and was stone cold. They must have knocked, but she had gone to sleep again. On the tray was a letter and a telegram. She opened the telegram, and read:

> Passed in both surgery and medicine.
>
> Roy

For a moment Beatrice could not believe her eyes. Roy had passed! A great weight fell from her heart, and for once in her life Beatrice burst into tears.

What could it mean? Had Roy been capable of playing a trick on her? Had he been lying there shamming?

She sprang up, laughing; then, glancing at the letter she held in her hand, saw that it was addressed to her in Roy's handwriting. On the envelope was scrawled in indelible pencil, "Insufficiently addressed. Not known at St. Xavier's College, try St. Xavier's Hospital." Roy had written "St. Xavier's, London." The letter must be several days old. Beatrice opened it, and read:

My dear Beatrice,

"I am afraid what I write will hurt you frightfully, but I feel that I must be quite open and honest with you at all costs. I must tell you that I am not in love with you; as you know, I love you and always have loved you, and I think I always shall, as much as one can love a person with whom one is not passionately in love. I thought my love would suffice when I asked you to marry me. What is terrible is that I have now fallen in love with someone else. I find it has made no difference at all to my feelings for you, it has only made me unhappy because I am hurting you. Your feelings will probably be quite changed to me now, and it is for you to determine whether our old comradeship can continue in any form, or whether that would be too painful for you.

"I have been most hideously to blame, and I shall never forget all that you have done for me. No one ever has done as much for anybody as you have done for me. I do not know whether I have any chance with the person I am in love with, but I must ask you to break off our engagement, as marriage with you is impossible while I am liable to feel like this for someone else.

Yours ever,
Roy Gordon

Beatrice folded the letter, and put it back into the envelope. She had dreaded this, had secretly known yet had never admitted it, or quite faced it.

She had really known, had always known that Roy was not in love with her. Now he was in love with somone else, and he had found it out himself.

The blow had fallen, but for the first moment it hurt her less than she had expected. She felt she had nothing to reproach Roy with. It was as much her fault as his. She knew that she loved Roy passionately, that she could never care for anybody else, but she felt from her letter that she had not completely lost him. Too painful for her to go on seeing him! What an absurd idea. She had accustomed herself to the pain of seeing him and being in love with him since she was a little girl: when he had proposed to her a year ago, she had accepted the idea of their marriage, but she felt it was a dream, too good to be true, and she felt that Roy's feelings hadn't changed at all. He had always felt like that, and he had only got engaged to her because he knew how happy it would make her.

Compared with what she had thought the evening before, the pain of this was nothing. Roy had passed his examination. Suddenly she remembered that Roy was lying there close by sleeping off the effects of his drunkenness. Well, she could forgive that, knowing that he had passed his exam, and that he hadn't meant to leave her for three days without a word of explanation.

She hurried down, and learnt to her surprise that Roy had woken up a couple of hours before, had been perfectly collected, and had been allowed to go home.

When she got back to her room she found him waiting for her. He was standing, and gave her a quick glance.

"Oh, I'm so glad, Roy, I'm so glad. I've only just had the telegram."

"Oh Lord—I sent it last night."

Roy saw her coming towards him with outstretched hands, and caught her in his arms, and gave her not a kiss, but a good hug. He let her go at once, and walked away to the window. She looked at him keenly, and unconsciously he answered her thought.

"Beatrice, do you know how I came here last night?"

"Did you come here?"

"I woke up here this morning."

"Oh?"

"Well, if you won't tell me—"

"The police brought you in."

"Was I drunk?"

Beatrice looked at him, and found that he was serious.

"Yes," she answered, "dead drunk."

"How beastly of me," said Roy, rather airily, and appeared to think the subject closed, for he went on:

"Beatrice—can you bear to see me ever again?"

"If you're sober, otherwise I'll tell the police to cart you off." She found she could laugh.

"You are a dear. Oh, Beatrice, it's not simple at all."

"I got your letter, but only this morning."

"What?" Roy was horrified.

"They sent it to St. Xavier's College."

"How ghastly. Then you didn't know anything?"

"Not a word. Now, sit down, and tell me everything. I can bear it, you know," said Beatrice, with a kind of stoical resolution which she had always had from a child. "Tell me about Claire."

"It's dreadful about her," said Roy.

"Won't she have you, is she married already, or what?"

"Claire and I are going to be married."

"Anything else?"

Roy was looking away out of the window with a desperate, troubled look on his face. At last, he said in a low voice:

"She is a cocaine fiend."

Beatrice whistled. She said nothing. After a few minutes, Roy went on:

"Stand by me, Beatrice, help me pull her through. I can't bear to see it. She's killing herself. It's simply horrible."

"How long has she been taking it?"

"Nearly two years. Since she was sixteen."

"What a shame! What a beastly shame!" Beatrice cried the words out passionately, angrily.

To give a girl of sixteen cocaine! Beatrice stood rigid with anger, and all that was best in her generous nature came uppermost. Claire was forgotten as her rival, forgotten as a danger for Roy; for only a moment before Beatrice had hated her because she felt instinctively that Claire would never make Roy happy. She would ruin Roy's life. Beatrice would have counted her own happiness for little if she had known Roy was going to be happy, but what would come but the most horrible disaster if Roy were to marry a druggist—a slave to one of those awful alkaloids that poison the body, intoxicate the brain, and silently, secretly steal away the will-power of their victims?

A moment before she had felt this, and hated Claire, but when Roy with that despairing look had told her Claire had been given cocaine when she was sixteen, Beatrice's feelings changed to pity and tenderness for Claire, and an angry hate for a world where such things can happen, where creatures live who would give cocaine to a mere child, very likely not from motives of fiendish wickedness to wreck her life, but from curiosity, from mere folly, for their amusement, or because they took it themselves, and yet could feel less remorse when they thought of the future and their own fate, if they knew that the same fate was in store for other people: they would all one day take an overdose or else die mad. Hate for such a world possessed her. And Beatrice stood there, with her whole being charged with hate for a world where such things are possible, and said again: "What a shame! What a shame! What devils people are!"

She looked at Roy, and suddenly saw tears were falling from his eyes on to the floor, where they splashed like drops of rain. He did not try and wipe them away and rub his eyes with his hands, but sat silent.

After a little while, she saw that his tears had stopped, but he still sat motionless, gazing past her out of the window.

"Tell me what happened last night," she suggested, to change the subject.

"I sent you a telegram about six, and then I met Claire, and we had dinner. I was very tired, and I really wanted to go home; but she took me to a party, and made me dance. I felt rather ill about one o'clock in the morning, and they gave me a glass of brandy. Then she said we had better go home, and we left. That's all I know."

"You only had one glass of brandy?"

"Yes. Nothing else all the evening. It—it wasn't by any chance cocaine?"

"Good Lord, no! Your heart. . ." began Beatrice in explanation. Then, "You don't mean to say you had some, and that I didn't diagnose it?"

"No. I tell you I don't remember anything about it. I hadn't had any sleep the night before, and not very much the night before that.

"That explains the mystery," said Beatrice. "You were simply dead beat. A tablespoonful of brandy will do it if you are sufficiently exhausted."

"Where was I picked up?"

"In Francis Street."

Roy nodded.

"Her friends were, I think, somewhere near Gower Street; perhaps it was Gordon Square. I must have simply lain down."

Beatrice reflected that Claire must have simply left him lying in the street, but kept her thought to herself.

"How on earth you passed your exam!"

"Oh, that was easy, as it turned out," said Roy. "I didn't have a hitch anywhere; they were pleased with me; but, of course, it's a strain, and—I was a good deal worried about you and Claire. I couldn't sleep. I took some bromide, but it was no good at all; it isn't, you know, in those cases."

She nodded.

"Well, Roy, I'll help you all I can. I mean if it's any good, always come and talk to me. It was quite as much my fault as yours we got engaged; in fact, you weren't to blame in the least."

"Good-bye, Beatrice."

"Good-bye, Roy."

They shook hands at parting. When he had gone, Beatrice stood for a few minutes by the window reflecting. Her face looked harder, leaner, with its strong jaw thrust out. She thought over all that Roy had told her.

"Cocaine's the devil!" she cried out, savagely, in a loud voice, and picking up a Venetian glass vase threw it into the fender, where it smashed. She burst into tears, and sobbed desperately, as if her heart would break.

DAVID GARNETT

VII

At eighteen, Claire Plowman's mind and character were already completely formed. She had had varied and horrible experiences, and had contracted one of the most terrible vices in the world. Sniffing cocaine is the most terrible, the most dangerous and horrible habit that can be formed. The devotees of cocaine all end under sentence of early death. In a girl of Claire's age there is practically no hope.

When Roy met her Claire was living a most extraordinary life. She had been left a very large sum of money, and for the first time in her life she could do exactly as she pleased. At Brighton she had been in the power of a man whom she hated, otherwise she would have lost her job. The only thing that enabled her to go on with such an existence was the drug which the girl she met in Regent Street had originally given her, and the fact that he was not often there—Walter Bangham, actor, theatrical agent and dope-fiend was a big, ugly man who had made his way in business by sheer brutality. He bullied everyone over whom he had power, and by a bluff heartiness of manner made himself the crony of his employers.

Fortunately for Claire she was at that time too insignificant for him to pay much attention to her, besides which his main business was in London, so that in the eighteen months before his death, when Claire knew him, she had only seen him a dozen times. On the last occasion he had tied her to the foot of his bed and beat her with the strap of his Gladstone bag until she fell limp and unconscious, foaming at the mouth.

When the old man whose life she had saved when she was a little girl of twelve died, and whom she had deserted in his old age, left her his money—eleven thousand pounds, Claire came to London and took rooms in a hotel. She knew a certain number of actors and actresses and soon had a wide circle of acquaintances. Most of the men tried to marry her because she had money, but Claire would have nothing to say to them. Those men who tried to make love to her did not repeat the experiment. What she had told Roy was strictly true; she had never been in love before in her life, and though she enjoyed making men go mad about her, she had no wish to have love affairs with them. Living, as she did, in the loosest company, she was a novelty, and in the three months before she met Roy, Claire became something of a celebrity.

She was always asked to all the parties given in the flashy Bohemian world in which she moved. No dance, gambling party, or secret doping orgy was complete without her. Under the effect of cocaine, which she took more and more recklessly, she became inspired with a wild frenzy, and danced like a Bacchante, drank off a bottle of champagne, and played a thousand wild antics.

She was absolutely without fear, and even fond of danger. One night reeling about the floor of the night club, she bet anyone five pounds she would get out of the window and sit on the ledge outside while the window was shut behind her, and there uncork a bottle of champagne and drink it off without taking it from her lips. A German count took her bet, and Claire climbed out, with a bottle and a pair of nippers in her hand. A hundred men and women drawn from all classes of society crowded round to watch her and not one had the decency to interfere. Claire drank the champagne, and then smashed a hole in the window and threw the bottle into the room, hitting the German on the head. All she lived for was excitement and sensation. Yet though she was fond of luxury and was happiest in insane orgies, she clung to some things with determination. One of these was her love of music. She would go anywhere to hear a good performer. She never sang anything herself but old English airs, and though she was quite untrained, had a really beautiful voice and good taste. When she first saw Roy in the night club she fell in love with him at first sight, chiefly because of his looks. He was probably the only man she had ever met who was really gentle and refined. He took his place as naturally as a king. Roy never pushed himself to the front. He was simply there.

VIII

Roy and Claire were married three weeks after they first met. They spent the interval in taking a house and furnishing it. After some hesitation they selected an old house in Chiswick, with a garden stretching down to the river. Claire had persuaded Roy to put off going into practice. They had a thousand a year between them, and he need be in no hurry earn money before he wanted to.

Roy and Claire were both naturally extravagant, and for some days thoroughly enjoyed themselves in choosing luxurious carpets and expensive furniture. The largest room in their new house opened with double windows into the garden. There was a huge concert grand piano at one end, and a long dining table at the other. They bought the best of everything—rugs, chairs, cushions. Roy, of course, had a good many things—the Gordon family silver, and a priceless collection of pictures. The curtains were of heavy Chinese silk. Claire insisted on the utmost luxury everywhere around her, but in one thing, her dress, she was simplicity itself. She understood, by some queer instinct, that her extraordinary fresh beauty could never be more striking than when she was plainly dressed in a simple muslin frock.

Jewels, or splendid gowns, simply looked incongruous when she wore them. Anyone who did not know her might have mistaken her for a housemaid going out on her afternoon off. But Claire spent a Small fortune on her shoes. By another of Claire's freaks their bedroom was simplicity itself, plainly whitewashed, and with a few pieces of good old furniture, it might have been the best bedroom in an eighteenth century farmhouse

For the first fortnight Claire threw herself into furnishing the house with the greatest energy, but a few days before their marriage a curious change came over her. She seemed to have lost her interest in everything, and to be rather dull and listless, and she complained to Roy of headaches.

Roy was secretly extremely uneasy. The way in which she had given up cocaine, and had never made any reference to it, had surprised him a good deal. It was an almost incredible instance of will-power in anyone addicted to drugs, and Roy was made to feel extraordinarily happy by it. He could scarcely believe in so easy a victory.

However, there was no question about it—Claire had given up drugs. Now she was beginning to suffer, but Roy felt if he could nurse her through a few more weeks they would be safe. Her character seemed to have undergone a change too. She became awkward and shy, and sometimes Roy could hardly believe that she was the brilliant creature whom he had danced with, and whose fierce personality had drawn applause from everybody in the room. She was gentle, and timid of the new servants, and the pains in her head grew worse; she lost her colour, and seemed sometimes almost plain.

However, the day of their marriage passed on quietly, and Claire recovered some of her old gaiety, but on the second day after it she was seized with violent pain and could not get up.

Roy left her in bed and went to have a bath, and while he was standing at the window drying himself he suddenly saw Claire in her pyjamas wheeling a barrow at the bottom of the garden. Roy was so much surprised that for the first moment he could scarcely believe his senses. The next moment she had stepped into the barrow, and from it was able to reach the top of the garden wall that lay between them and the river. Roy saw her scramble up, but without waiting longer dashed downstairs and out into the garden.

Claire had vanished!

In three seconds Roy was on top of the wall, and in a fourth had taken a header into the river. The tide was high, and it had just turned and was running fast down-stream, and Claire was already forty yards off. But Roy had not wasted his time at Cambridge. Just before he came up with her she was carried under for the third or fourth time.

Roy emptied his lungs and struck down. His eyes were open, but in the foul Thames water he could scarcely see. He sank rapidly, swimming hard. Suddenly he touched something, saw something. It was white. It was Claire. Together they were whirled along, but with bursting lungs he brought her at last up to the surface. She was choking, but began breathing again as he swam with her to the bank.

He brought her home in his arms. All that day she lay in bed, banked with hot water bottles, in a half-comatose condition.

In the evening she appeared better, and ate greedily. She scarcely seemed to recognise Roy, and insisted on getting up and dressing.

"I must go," she said. She was savage, and absolutely set on leaving the house.

"I must get cocaine, or I shall kill myself," she said sullenly. "If you keep me here I shall bite my hand off."

Her rosy colour had all gone, and she looked at him with fixed eyes, with the pupils shrunk up to mere points.

When she was dressed she said to Roy, who had locked the door and put the key in his pocket:

"Open the door. If I don't get cocaine tonight I shall go mad. You can't do more than I've done myself."

As Roy thought to himself that it was quite possible that she would, as she said, go mad, he opened the door and gave her a few drops of laudanum in warm water.

While he was getting it ready Claire walked about with her teeth chattering and her eyes rolling wildly. She was scarcely conscious. The laudanum had no effect as a sleeping draught, on the contrary it seemed to make her more lively.

"Give me cocaine," she snarled at him like a wild beast.

For half an hour she lay panting and shivering violently. Then she began gnashing her teeth and making hardly intelligible noises. Roy opened the door and took her with him to the small room he had fitted up as a surgery and kept locked. He gave her an injection of morphine.

Slowly the colour came back into Claire's face. The fixed look vanished from her eyes, they sparkled slightly; a moment later she smiled, and running to him clung to him like a frightened child. Putting her hands up to his shoulders with queer, confiding gestures, she looked at him, seeming to entreat his forgiveness.

He picked her up and carried her to their room. She nestled close to him in bed, pressing her young body tightly against his, and holding him still tightly in her arms, sighed heavily and fell asleep. Roy's head was aching. He felt absolutely at breaking-point, full of a dull pain. The shock had been awful for him, and his heart was heavy with sorrow. At last, he too fell asleep.

At four o'clock in the morning Claire woke him rather roughly. It was already nearly light. He had forgotten to draw the curtains overnight.

"Give me some dope, darling."

He pulled himself together and sat up, rubbing his eyes.

Claire was looking at him with clear, candid eyes, like those of a child.

"Get me some cocaine. Please—darling." Claire came closer and slipped her hands round just under his pyjama jacket.

"Don't you see it's ruin? It's fatal. You'll never give it up. My darling creature, if you can possibly endure it you must stand it; if you will bear it for another week you'll never want it again."

"Please, darling, I must have it."

This scene lasted for two hours. Roy won.

By next evening Claire had become very restless, and Roy was at the end of his strength. He had been watching her every movement all day. At dinner Claire wouldn't eat anything, and couldn't sit still. She kept taking things up and putting them down again. Then she suddenly went up to him and said in a low voice:

"Roy, I shall die if you don't let me have cocaine. I shall die. I've been taking a lot until I met you. I know I am going to die. If you give it me we shall be happy for two or three years. I may last five years if you give it to me. Five years of happiness, that's not to be despised."

"No—you can't have it, and I tell you as a doctor you'll live," said Roy. However, he did not feel sure of it.

Claire began walking about again, picking things up and putting them down.

Suddenly he saw that a crisis was upon them. Claire darted a look of rage and hatred at him and dashed out of the room and out of the house. Roy caught her up at the corner of the street. He was horrified by her appearance. Nothing had yet been so horrible. Her face was convulsed with rage, distorted beyond recognition. She gnashed her teeth like an animal in a trap, and rolled her eyes wildly.

"Let me go, let me go! I shan't live with you. You can't make me live with you. Let me go. I can't stand it—Oh, I hate you—you devil!"

Roy held her against a wall, and Claire began cursing him.

It's only a question of time, he thought to himself, and if we go on like this she will die or kill herself. I've no legal right to keep her against her will. . .

"I'll give you some cocaine," he said wearily.

But Claire answered him: "I shan't come and live with you any more. You don't know what it means, you don't know what I suffer." She seemed calmer.

"Come back on any terms," said Roy.

"No, I can't go on like this; it'll kill you too." She paused, and then said: "I would if you loved me and understood. Give me some coc. now and take some yourself."

Roy nodded. He was almost amused at the last request. What did it matter to him what happened to him? He knew also that he would never fall a victim to a habit, and that if he once made up his mind he could always break himself of any habit he formed.

DAVID GARNETT

They walked back in silence.

When I've won her love completely, in six months' time, I'll try again. If I've got myself to cure at the same time I shall know more about it, Roy thought to himself.

He gave her a pill-box filled with the white powder, and she snuffed it greedily. He took a pinch himself.

"Not too much at first," she cautioned him. She was still solemn. It did not seem the drug had much effect on her. It had none he could detect on himself except that it felt cold as it evaporated in his nostrils. That was all.

"Now let's have dinner or something," said Claire. She was smiling, but seemed rather shy.

His heart began to beat faster, his eyes sparkled. Claire had never before looked so lovely, so wonderful, so adorable.

"Come here," he said. She came to him with an almost passionate reasonableness.

"Roy, darling, don't take it again. It's wicked. I don't know what I'm doing. I can't stop. Promise me you won't take it again?"

"No," said Roy, kissing her. "I promise you that I shall. The only person I care for in the world is you. All I ever want is your happiness. Let us be happy for three months—then we'll try again."

Claire looked at him like an angel from Heaven.

There were tears in her eyes.

IX

The following weeks Beatrice underwent all the agony of realising her position.

At first, sheer unselfish love for Roy had triumphed over her personal unhappiness. She had put her jealousy, her despair from her. She had pretended to herself that she had not lost Roy completely, and that while they still had their work in common they could go on seeing each other and being friends. She told herself that that relation with Roy was so precious to her that it should content her.

But after his marriage the weeks went by and Beatrice heard nothing from Roy. She forced herself to accept the bitter truth. She had lost Roy; anything else was a mockery and a delusion. So Beatrice went grimly about her work with her strong face set, taciturn and untiring. When she was happy Beatrice was fond of companionship, but in her dark hours she shut herself up and saw no one. Her only distraction was work, her only way of escape from herself was work. She had never confided her disappointments to anyone, she had no wish for the sympathy of others. She was cast in the stoic mould.

Beatrice did not hear anything of Roy or Claire for six weeks. During that time she scarcely left the hospital, and was always, if possible, in the wards. When she went out she avoided going anywhere where she was likely to meet Roy or Claire. When she did hear, it was not from Roy, but, to her surprise, from Claire.

The letter, in an ungainly hand, ran:

> Bur et Tanac, Cornwall
>
> Dear Miss Chase,
>
> Roy has to go to Dundee to bury his uncle. I want to know you, and this seems a good opportunity. Can you come down for the week, and if you like stay on after Roy comes back? Yours, very sincerely, Claire Gordon.

Beatrice looked at it grimly. She could find nothing to take exception to, except an indifference to the fate of Roy's uncles; an indifference which Beatrice could hardly complain of for she knew them, and shared it herself. She wired acceptance. As she had been free to take a holiday for the last two months, there was no difficulty in leaving the hospital.

The evening following she arrived at a small station in Cornwall and found a motor car waiting for her. The driver explained that he could only take her part of the way. They drove for an hour through the wildest country Beatrice had ever seen, and then pulled up at a bend in the road. Beatrice got out and walked up a winding path pointed out by the driver.

A figure, probably Claire, was coming to meet her. As she approached, Beatrice saw it was a village girl of about fourteen. She was bare-legged, with her feet thrust into sand-shoes, bare-headed, with two golden plaits of hair hanging on her shoulders. She was dressed in a short skirt and a white sailor jumper that left her throat and her chest bare. Beatrice took her in, as she came towards her, against a background of flaming yellow gorse, and suddenly realised that it was Claire after all.

She came up to her and said:

"How do you do?" but, rather to Beatrice's relief, did not kiss her, or even offer to shake hands.

"Let me carry your bag," said Claire, and on her refusing, took it by main force. "It's over the top, down this way by the sea."

They turned to one side, and Beatrice saw a small cottage standing alone on the edge of the most savage cliff she had ever seen. There was a tiny beach below, a boat drawn up, and the murmur of the sea came to her ears.

"Do you like it?" asked Claire.

"Yes, it is a good place," Beatrice answered. She felt rather awed by the beauty of her surroundings.

"I'm so glad. That's our boat." Claire pointed. "We usually go out all day fishing. Can you swim? I can't. Roy is teaching me."

The cottage was tiny. Roy and Claire had come there a fortnight after their marriage.

"We're quite alone—not even the baker; I make the bread. We fetch all our groceries round by water."

Claire showed Beatrice a tiny room.

"That's your room, though if you do as we do you'll hardly ever use it, we sleep down on the beach and have all our meals out. It hasn't rained once since we've been here. Isn't that wonderful?"

Beatrice found herself liking the girl. It was possible that she might be rather a bore, but one couldn't help liking her, she was so simple, so extraordinarily lovely, and so unconscious of her own charm.

Claire brought their supper out on to a table within a yard of the edge of the cliff.

"If you sit on that side and push your chair back you go over," said Claire; "that's how the ravens get fed in the wilderness. They've got a nest down there."

Beatrice found she was amused. Claire wouldn't be a bore. She took her things down and slept with Claire on the beach.

For two days Beatrice lived there perfectly happily with Claire, and couldn't help growing fond of her. They went out all day, sailing and fishing, and Beatrice was astonished at the way in which Claire had learnt to handle the boat. Sometimes she would take it in within a foot of the sheer face of rock, and put about calmly just as Beatrice thought they were going to be crushed like an eggshell. On the second occasion that this happened Beatrice asked Claire why she did it.

"Roy says if one wants mullets one ought to go in under the cliffs," she explained.

The third day they woke up to find the sky overcast and a strong wind blowing. Claire was taciturn and gloomy during breakfast. Beatrice put it down to the weather. She was surprised Claire should take it so unphilosophically, though it was annoying; they had talked of going round the coast to a village which Claire hadn't yet visited.

Soon afterwards it came on to rain, and Beatrice went to her room. When she went into the kitchen she found Claire dressed in a jersey and with Roy's rubber fishing boots that came up to her thighs. She was carrying a treacle tin in her hand.

"If I don't come back you'll be here to look after Roy. You'd better marry him, you know," and Claire went out into the rain. Beatrice went to the door.

"Hi!" she called. Claire turned round.

"What's the matter, Claire?"

"Nothing."

"Where are you going?"

Claire turned round and began walking down to the beach. Beatrice looked after her. Yes, Claire was going out in the boat. She saw her straining to push it down to the water; or was she going to pull it up higher? No, she meant to go out.

Beatrice ran out on to the cliff and shouted, but the wind carried her words down her throat. She waited a moment in doubt, then ran down the path to the beach. Quite big waves were rolling in, it was a dangerous beach studded with rocks, and Beatrice felt sure that Claire would never get the boat out through the rollers; if she did, it was a hundred to one it would be carried on to a rock and smashed up. A turn in the path, shut Claire and the boat out of view, and when Beatrice got on to the beach she found Claire had pushed the boat out through the first breakers and was clinging to it, up to her waist in water.

The water receded, dragging the boat and Claire with it. Now it was not up to her knees, and the boat was almost aground. A great wave came rushing in, for a second it seemed to hang over the end of the boat. In that second Beatrice saw Claire vault into the stern and the wave break in a smother of foam. It swept the boat in nearer. For a moment they were quite close to each other. Claire had seized an oar and was poling the boat out again.

Beatrice shouted as loud as she could and Claire yelled something back. All she could catch was:

"Burn me. . . Shelley."

Another wave broke over them, and for a second the boat vanished. The next instant Beatrice saw it riding further out. Another wave, and there was Claire hoisting the sail. She saw the whole thing reel over, and water pour in over the side; then it righted, and they were off like an arrow.

"Well, if she hits a rock, I can't do anything, though I suppose I shall have to try," Beatrice said to herself. After a few minutes she mounted the cliff to get a better view.

"What a little Tartar! I suppose she thought me a funk for writing letters!"

The day wore on and Claire did not return, and although the rain and mist cleared off and the sun came out, the wind freshened and the waves grew bigger. Beatrice grew more and more anxious. Had Claire, she wondered, intended to commit suicide? Since she had not come in she must be drowned, or carried right out to sea.

Towards evening she wrapped herself up in a thick coat and sat on the cliff edge. She smoked cigarette after cigarette, and for once in her life could not find refuge from her anxieties in work. She could not help watching. The sun had set when at last a tiny speck became visible. It grew and grew, it was certainly a boat. It was Claire. Beatrice did not quite know what she felt, relief was certainly the strongest. She watched it pitching and falling, and slowly growing bigger for an hour. When she went down on the beach Claire was within fifty yards, and drove the boat through the breakers with unerring skill. It ran aground, and Claire leapt ashore, and began dragging the boat up.

Beatrice went and helped her. Claire was wet to the skin, and her hair was plastered on her neck with spray, her cheeks were fiery red, her eyes flashed with extraordinary brightness. She seemed to be in wild spirits.

"Have you had a good time?" Beatrice asked her.

"I've never been so sick in my life," and Claire laughed, hilariously, showing two rows of dazzling teeth.

They went up to the house. Claire changed her clothes, while Beatrice made the supper. They had it indoors.

"There ought to be some champagne somewhere," said Claire.

Beatrice advised hot rum and lemon.

"There's brandy."

Claire poured out a glass, filled it up with hot water, and drank it off. When they had finished their meal, Claire sat in front of the fire drying her hair.

"Roy told you I take cocaine?" Claire asked.

"Yes, but I thought you'd given it up."

Claire laughed. She was diabolically pretty at that moment.

"Well, I thought I would try and stop, and that it was a good opportunity now Roy is away, but it won't do. You saw what I was like this morning. No, probably you didn't see. I went out with a matchbox full in that old tin to keep it dry, and when I got some way out I wondered—Shall I drown, or shall I take some coc? Then I was sick, awfully sick, and the sun came out. Such gorgeous colours you never saw in the water, and the noise of the water was lovely. I was being sick all the time, you understand, but I thought I'd rather go on living a bit longer, it was all so lovely, so I opened the tin and took some. About half of it blew away at each sniff."

Beatrice looked at her with a feeling of cold horror. She could see now that Claire had been taking some drug: her brilliant colour, glittering eye, and her excitement, all proclaimed it. And Beatrice had thought it was simply the effect of the wind and rain! That child, she reflected, had been tossing up and down all day in a cockleshell in a raging sea doping herself! It was too ghastly.

"Does Roy know you still take it?" she asked, though, of course, Roy must know, she reflected, directly she had asked the question.

"Yes." Claire paused. "I like you, Beatrice. Now listen. I'm hopeless.

I've tried my hardest, and Roy thinks he's tried. He knows I'm hopeless. I guess I've about two more years to run. Three at the outside. Then I shall go cracky or kill myself. Now Roy. . ." She looked away. "Roy is taking it a bit now, off and on. He can stop when he likes. I swear I don't want him to take it. In two years' time he'll be as bad as I am if he gets into the way of it. Make him stop. You see, Beatrice, I can't help myself. Sometimes I want him to take it. It makes him understand so. It brings him so close, and then he's mine; but I don't want to hurt Roy. When I'm dead, he'll be yours, so look after him."

Claire was breathing quickly in short gasps, and looked at Beatrice in a scared way.

"That's what I wanted to say to you."

But Beatrice sat silent. She had propped her face on her clenched fist, and was staring in front of her. She saw that what Claire had told her was true.

Roy was taking cocaine! Probably what Claire said about her own case was true, and that she was hopeless. Short of keeping her in a strait waistcoat and forcibly feeding her for a month, there was probably nothing for it, and even then she would quite likely go mad. Roy is taking cocaine, Beatrice repeated over and over to herself, Roy is taking cocaine.

Presently a faint cry came from Claire. Beatrice looked at her. Claire was breathing in a peculiar, rhythmic way. Beatrice considered her for a moment, while Claire gazed at her with her bright, glittering eyes.

"I think I've done it this time," she articulated, in a hardly audible whisper. Beatrice felt her pulse, and at once got up. Claire had obviously taken an overdose.

Beatrice picked her up, and laid her on the bed.

Roy is taking cocaine, she said over and over to herself, as she set to work on Claire. It never occurred to her that she might simply let Claire die. By three o'clock in the morning Beatrice thought Claire was out of danger, and would pull round all right by herself, so she lay down fully dressed on her own bed, and fell fast asleep.

X

The next day, when Beatrice woke, she found Claire was already up and about; the sun was high in the heavens, and everything had that wonderful freshness that comes on summer mornings after rain. She went out of the cottage, and found Claire waiting for her: breakfast was ready.

Beatrice felt that the previous day, with all that had happened in it, her long dreary watch upon the cliffs, Claire's awful confession and her sudden illness, was far away. It seemed like some terrible nightmare that could have no connection with the world as she now saw it—the shining strip of sand below, the blue sea, the clear sun-pervaded spaces of the air, where white birds wheeled lazily, dipped to the seashore, and mounted in spirals to the highest rocks. How lovely it was! When the world was so beautiful, when it was such a good place to live in, how could anything vile or ugly exist? Beatrice looked at Claire, and sighed. Nothing was so lovely as the girl sitting before her there on the cliff's edge. She was a picture of childish grace and innocence.

Claire had dressed herself in a simple, clean print frock, her colour was perfect, and her face was full of innocent repose. It was difficult to imagine that a few hours before she had been lying unconscious, with dilated eyes and distorted features. When she saw Beatrice, Claire rose and came to her and kissed her. Beatrice sat down with a troubled heart.

All that day Claire could not do too much for her. They did not go out in the boat.

In the afternoon a telegram came from Roy to say that he would be back that evening. Claire did not seem to be pleased, and as the afternoon wore on Beatrice found herself feeling unaccountably nervous. She wondered if it would not have been better to have gone back to London without waiting for Roy. And Beatrice asked herself over and over again whether she could have it out with Roy about his taking this drug. She felt she must speak to him, but she felt also that it was not her business. She knew Roy well enough to know that he did not do things without a reason, and that he fiercely resented any interference. Still, she must speak.

He came half-an-hour before they expected him, and found them preparing the evening meal. He waved a newspaper at Beatrice, and walked up to Claire and kissed her, held her for a moment to gaze at her with a searching expression, as if he would read the history of the last few days in her lovely face.

"War's declared," he said.

That evening things seemed to go all right, as they could discuss the war, and what was likely to happen.

"You must join the army," said Beatrice, "they'll want all the doctors they can get."

"If you join, you must be a common swaddy," said Claire. "You mustn't leave me to go and be a doctor." She looked sulky, and was obviously ready to be jealous of Beatrice. A moment later, she said:

"I'm going down on the beach," and, gathering her things up, went out of the room, robed in blankets.

Roy watched her go, his lean face had seemed to Beatrice more sensitive, more civilised, than ever. The tenderness of his smile, the slightly mocking look of love and admiration in the eyes revealed suddenly just how Roy could care as he did for Claire, seeing all her faults, the horror of her doping habit and doped moods, and only loving her the more tenderly for her imperfections and her vice.

"Dear old Roy," said Beatrice. Her heart was full, and she had never felt so near breaking down. She found he was looking at her.

"Will you take the morning train?"

Roy had risen, and was getting his blankets. She found she had not said any of the important things. It was her last chance. Roy had told her to go. No doubt he was afraid of a scene, and she felt ashamed of having stayed. It came over her that Claire had not asked her to stay since her letter. Roy was in the doorway holding a lantern; in a moment he would be gone.

"Roy. . . don't take cocaine."

He turned round at once, and she saw him considering her gravely.

"Roy, it's too dreadful. Claire told me she didn't want you to. She asked me to stop you."

Still Roy did not speak. Beatrice rose, and cried out suddenly:

"I see now it's true. You have no courage, Roy. You always do the easiest thing, you give up Claire's case and tell her it's hopeless, and dope yourself. You're weak, weak, weak. You'd certainly better not go into the army; Heaven help you if you were a soldier!"

Roy had turned round to face her, and stood in the open doorway against the black gulf that was sea and sky. He said nothing; he seemed to wait in patient resignation for her to say something more biting still.

"Roy, what possessed you to marry that woman? It wasn't as if you had to. It was just weakness—it was the easiest way to get what you wanted. If you had cured her there might be something to be said, even so it was idiotic. She's very pretty, and she isn't self-seeking; in fact, I like her, but there's nothing really remarkable about her except that she takes drugs. She's one of the great army of prostitutes drawn from the lower classes. She's no brains. You'll never have any children by her, and when she's dead you'll never have children by any one else. When she's dead, you'll go into a nursing home and tinker with cures, and look shifty, and die suddenly from an overdose of some vile substitute. Last night Claire said she was hopeless, and in a year or two she would die, and you would be mine. No, thank you, Roy. I shan't want you then. I don't want to see you again. I hate being reminded of my mistakes. I don't care for weaklings."

She paused, and, swallowing a lump in her throat, went on:

"Still, as a doctor, I'll tell you what you must know yourself. Claire is as good as dead. She may live two or three years if she's careful, but I doubt if she'll live six months. You have taken to doping yourself with her example in front of your eyes. If you do it now, I expect you'll always do it. There will be plenty of reasons for you to go on. I don't want to have anything more to do with you, but I tell you for your own good that you've only one chance. It's the advice any doctor would give you. Put Claire into a home. She may die, she may live, she'll probably go mad, but, as you know, there is an off-chance she'll recover. Join the army. That's all I've got to say. I don't want to speak to you again."

Beatrice had looked away from Roy while she had been making this speech, and sat with her eyes on the ground.

Suddenly, she heard a faint movement, and, looking up, saw that Claire was standing behind Roy, and had put her hand on his arm. She had heard all Beatrice had said.

"Come, darling, come down to the beach."

Roy stood as if lost in mazes of reflection and contemplation; he seemed to be thinking. It was as if what Beatrice had said had reminded him of some unsolved question, so that he had stood wrestling with memory and oblivious of what she had been saying, or that Claire's was there speaking to him. Claire's voice came again:

"I've never been so cruel as you, Beatrice. I've never tried to hurt Roy. You are unhappy, and you try and make everybody else unhappy. That's what I think cowardly. You'll live, Beatrice, long after I'm dead, and perhaps when Roy is dead, but I'm glad I'm not you. I asked you here because you loved Roy, and I wanted to be nice to you. I was nice to you. Last night. . . You are a devil, a cold-blooded devil, Beatrice; Roy and I will be happy together in spite of death, in spite of you. You'll never be happy, Beatrice, because you are a heartless, selfish, cold, cruel creature. I shan't have children, I know, but, my God, anybody would rather have me for a mother than you." Claire paused. She gave a sudden loud laugh that rang through the air.

Beatrice watched her, and Roy turned and put a restraining arm on Claire's shoulder. Claire had pulled out a gold box which she had hanging on a fine chain round her neck, and, opening it, dipped her finger in it. With extraordinary lightness, like a bird, she lifted her finger to each of Roy's nostrils, standing on tiptoe to do it.

"Come, darling, come down to the beach."

Roy turned and walked with her, and Beatrice was left staring after them into the darkness.

Outside in the night, Claire suddenly began singing in a clear, sweet voice:

> *"My flocks feed not,*
> *My ewes breed not,*
> *My rams speed not,*
> *All is amiss.*
>
> *Love's denying,*
> *Faith's defying,*
> *Heart's renying,*
> *Causer of this."*

Beatrice went to the window, and heard Claire's voice floating up from the winding path.

> *"Live with me, and be my love,*
> *And we will all the pleasures prove,*
> *That hills and valleys, dales and fields,*
> *And all the craggy mountains yields.*
>
> *There we will sit upon the rocks,*
> *And see the shepherds feed their flocks*

By shallow rivers, by whose falls
Melodious birds sing madrigals."

Beatrice saw the lantern moving on the beach, and two dark figures in the light of it.

Suddenly there was a flash of light on the horizon, then another. "Boom! Boom!"

They were firing guns out at sea. The arm of a searchlight leapt suddenly into the sky from the blackness of the sea below her, and raked the coast.

"Boom! Boom!"

Beatrice was gone in the morning soon after dawn, long before either Roy or Claire were stirring.

XI

That morning Roy and Claire saw destroyers passing and re-passing, and half-a-dozen German liners brought in under escort to be interned. A coastguard appeared on the cliff for the first time during their stay, and the day after he was replaced by a picket of Territorials. Roy and Claire went out for the day fishing, and ran round the rocky coast to Falmouth harbour. At the entrance, a shot was fired across their bows. Roy lowered the sail, and a motor boat dashed up to them and hailed them.

"Where are you from?"

"Bur et Tanac."

"Righto! Is that the cottage up on the cliff along by the Bur rocks? Nasty bit of coast. We've got mines here; run straight in. I say, have you heard the news? Six German dreadnoughts sunk in the North Sea. We've lost the "Orion." Gives one an appetite for lunch, eh, what?" and the motor boat turned and bore away.

In Falmouth Roy was told the same news by the agent who had let them the cottage.

"I heard it from a man who was told it at the wireless station at Poldhu."

As they left the harbour Claire steered the boat alongside one of the great German liners that had been brought in. A hundred heads greeted them, clamouring for news and newspapers. All the passengers were being kept on board, and no one was allowed to leave. They had heard nothing.

Roy shook his head and shrugged his shoulders, and they glided quickly past. When they got back they found fifty territorials camped along the top of the cliff. Next morning they began digging trenches. Claire and Roy looked at them while they had breakfast in front of the cottage. Another hundred yards would bring the trench to the spot where they were sitting.

"Let's go to London," said Roy.

Claire nodded. "Bathe first."

They went down to the beach and undressed, then waded out, while the soldiers put down their little entrenching tools to come and watch. Roy took Claire below the armpits and swam out with her. The sun played in her hair and the waves sparkled. The water was like green glass. Roy felt happy at that moment, and trouble that had been lying in his heart completely left him. He turned on his side and Claire turned to face him, her mouth was full of water. She spluttered and laughed, then put her hand on Roy's shoulder.

"I'm happy," he said. "I'm so happy; anything was worth this."

Claire laughed and gurgled. She was too happy in the new accomplishment of swimming to speak or think. Words were not for her. She let go and splashed him, and went under herself, to come up spluttering the next moment.

"Never mind," she laughed. "I'll duck you yet," and splashed again.

Roy emptied his lungs and dropped away through the water to pop up half a minute later beside her. She caught hold of him and kissed him.

"I thought you were drowned."

They struck out further.

When they got in they were cold and shivered horribly in the warm sun. Claire was quite blue, and her teeth chattered. She looked so ill, and was so long fumbling with her things that Roy picked her up and carried her all the way up the path to the cottage. After she had been thoroughly rubbed, had dressed and swallowed a tablespoonful of neat brandy, she declared she felt better, but she still shivered a good deal.

In the train she seemed better, but her mood had changed.

In London they settled down to their ordinary life, but thing went badly. Claire semed to have become strangely restless, and although she was continually taking cocaine, her irritation increased. Every evening she insisted on dining out and carrying Roy off to some party where they, could dance. She would never dance with anyone except Roy, would hardly talk to anyone else, and kept him always at her side. Roy wondered at first why she was so anxious to go to these parties since it was not to meet people, and she knew he would have preferred them to stay at home. But soon he came to understand what she was feeling, perhaps better than she understood it herself. She wanted to forget. She was deeply in love with him, but when they were alone together she brooded all the time over her vice, and all her happiness was spoilt by realising that she had not much longer to live.

She seemed to be in an increasingly bad state of health. Roy became more and more worried, and convinced that something must be done, but he said nothing.

One day she said to him,

"I'm going to reform. You're keeping something from me, Roy. You want to join the army, but you think it's mean to leave me."

Roy's face told her that she had guessed right.

"If you go straight off and do what you ought, I'll keep off cocaine for the duration of the war."

Roy put his name down on the waiting list of a famous Highland regiment that afternoon. He was told he would be called up in a fortnight. During that time Claire entirely gave up drugs and stayed at home. He suggested giving a grand farewell party, to which they invited all their friends and casual acquaintances. Rather to Roy's surprise she suggested asking Beatrice. When he protested that she wouldn't want to come, and that he didn't want to see her, Claire insisted.

"I expect she feels rotten about it by this time."

Nearly a hundred people turned up, the house was so full that people went out into the garden. Roy was in his uniform, and welcomed everyone. He secretly regretted the party, but determined to make the best of it.

To his surprise Beatrice appeared, with Brewer. She went up to Roy and said:

"I'm sorry." She would have gone on, but Roy forestalled her.

"This isn't the time to be sorry," and squeezing her hand tightly, went off to welcome someone else.

A few minutes later Claire came in, dressed in white pyjamas. She was looking wonderful. One glance told Beatrice that she had been taking drugs. The little gold box she had seen in Cornwall was hanging round her neck on a fine chain. Claire tucked it next the skin. She had no corsets, and was, in fact, really wearing nothing but her heavy silk pyjamas and swansdown dancing shoes.

She fluttered up to Roy and led him aside; a moment later he came back, and Beatrice had a sudden conviction that he had just taken cocaine.

The room was cleared and they began dancing. Claire danced first with one, then with another, and Roy went about drinking and talking.

Beatrice saw him drink off whisky after whisky. He came to her end of the room laughing and chatting with a heavy-bearded man.

"A drop of Scotch all round." He filled their glasses.

The dancing stopped, and a well-kown music-hall artiste sang "You made me love you."

Supper was served in the garden. It was illuminated with Chinese lanterns. Nearly a hundred people sat down to a supper of oysters, paté de foie, lobster salad, cold chicken, and hot mince pies, with Claire's favourite Zabaglionis to crown all. There were peaches and nectarines for dessert. They drank claret.

After supper the boisterousness of the guests increased, and Roy went round pressing everyone to drink more. He was more than a little tipsy himself, but the more he drank the more charmingly urbane he became. Drinking served merely to reveal the extraordinary refinement of his nature. Claire sang several songs, and called to Roy to come and dance with her. After the first turn or two he fell to the floor, and Brewer and another man carried him upstairs to bed.

By this time the pianist was hopelessly drunk, and several of the party did not seem to know what they were doing. Men and women looked at each other with fiery, intoxicated glances, and helped each other unsteadily into the garden, where they were lost to sight. Others lay down on sofas or in the corners of the room. A tall beauty with brown eyes, one of the actresses who had been singing came up and openly asked Claire for cocaine. Taking her gold box she began sniffing it and laughing hysterically.

It was an unparalleled orgy, but Beatrice stayed on more from the feeling that a sober person was required than for any other reason. The man at the piano had gone into the garden, probably to be sick. After some time he returned, and pouring himself out a couple of glasses of whisky began to play again. One or two couples began dancing. Claire jumped on to the table and danced a hornpipe, kicking the bottles right and left, and laughing wildly as they smashed on the floor. There was loud applause.

"Roy can do the sword dance," she cried out, springing down when the dance was over. "Go and fetch him someone." But she ran upstairs herself to find him. Five minutes later Roy walked after her into the room. He was very pale.

"The sword dance," Claire shouted. Everybody took up the cry.

Roy had taken off his coat and slippers and was in his stockinged feet. He picked up his plaid and wrapped it round him. Then he seized a chair, and jumping on it he fetched down two old Highland swords from over the door. They had been in his family for centuries. He crossed them, and when a circle had been formed, and the pianist had begun playing, he began dancing. He danced wonderfully, with extraordinary

DAVID GARNETT

neatness and precision, and at every moment introduced new steps and variations. After ten minutes Beatrice saw to her horror that the floor was dabbled in blood.

The pianist had become more and more uncertain, and now, taking a glass in each hand, began thumping the keys at random.

Roy sat down on the floor.

"It's that damned piper—piano I mean. He put me off it. It's nothing to matter. If someone else will play I'll go on."

Beatrice advanced, and helped him to a sofa. A sudden crash of glass made her look round.

Claire had rushed at the pianist, who was still thumping the keys with a glass in each hand, and picked up an oil lamp and smashed it down over him on to the piano.

In a moment the oil had run over the top of the piano and was dribbling down the keyboard, in the next it had caught fire and flared up to the ceiling.

Claire laughed triumphantly.

"I told you I'd stop you playing. Now, go on!"

People swarmed in from the garden to watch. The flames roared up from the works and the celluloid keys burnt fiercely. The flames licked the ceiling, and the veneer of the piano, crackling in layers, burned quickly. After a few minutes someone brought a bucket of water and threw it over the piano. The room filled with smoke.

Brewer and Beatrice carried Roy upstairs and laid him in the first bed they found. Then Beatrice went to Roy's little surgery and found what she wanted. When she came back she stitched up two deep cuts in Roy's foot.

It was already growing light when she went down again. People were lying asleep on the sofas. In the early morning light the room looked dreadful. It resembled a room in a Belgian chateau that had been looted by the Germans. The grand piano was a ghastly sight, with broken wires frothing out of a charred hulk; broken bottles and glasses, pools of wine and bloodstains covered the floor. The swords, naked, still red with Roy's blood, were lying in the fender.

Beatrice went into the garden. It was empty. The flower beds were littered with empty bottles. A stray cat was gnawing at a large, untouched ham. She went back to the surgery and looked through Roy's stock. All the drugs she could find—cocaine, morphine, opium, laudanum, heroin, chloral, veronal, trional—she took away and threw over the wall into the river.

Where was Claire? Beatrice penetrated upstairs in search of her. Several of the previous night's guests were lying asleep in different rooms. One room, which she recognised as Claire's, was empty, and while she was standing irresolutely a door opened and Claire came in from the bathroom in her dressing-gown. She was still slightly wet, and looked as fresh as if she were a dairymaid who had just got up to go milking.

When she saw Beatrice she laughed and came up and gave her her fresh cheek to kiss. Beatrice was so exhausted that she kissed it mechanically.

"How's Roy? Did you enjoy yourself? I did—it was sport. I wonder how many we shall be to breakfast? I think I'll go to bed now and get a little sleep. Would you like a bed? I expect they're all full; you can come in with me here."

Beatrice was too tired to protest effectively. She refused, but Claire laughingly made her undress, and tucked her up. Half an hour later the two girls were sound asleep in each other's arms.

XII

It was a lovely day in the June of the following year when Beatrice and Claire stopped short with exclamations of surprise at finding themselves face to face. They were in Regent Street; both had been shopping.

Claire was radiant, and her warm smile dispelled any hesitation that Beatrice might have had in speaking to her.

"Come my way—let's have tea together. . . What a happy chance. . . I was thinking of you only the other day." With these words Claire greeted her.

Beatrice was, however, more glad of the accidental meeting than Claire. She had heard little, and seen nothing of either Roy or Claire since the day after the memorable night when Roy had danced the sword dance. She knew that Roy had joined his regiment directly he had been well enough to walk, and that he had gone out to France three months later. She had seen his regiment mentioned several times in despatches. That was all. At Christmas she had sent him a hamper, but had had no reply.

Often she had been tempted to write him a long letter, begging him to write to her; at any cost to her pride she would have been glad for their friendship to have been resumed. But when she sat down she had found it too hard to write. Beatrice found it was hard to judge Roy, but while he was taking drugs she felt too many conflicting emotions in her heart; what she had said on that terrible night of the 4th of August 1914 often seemed to her the truth. She could understand and pity Claire; she could in a sense like her; but Roy seemed to fall so far short of all that she had believed him to be. He was a weakling; he was led by his passion; he was a slave to the woman with whom he was in love.

Yet she could not forget his good qualities—his generosity, his readiness to sacrifice himself. Sometimes when she thought of Roy Beatrice felt her conscience sting her: had she perchance failed in what he had once asked her? He had asked her before his marriage to help him, to stand by him. No, she had not done that, but then why had Roy taken to drugs? She had not bargained for that. That was unpardonable. Beatrice wished bitterly that she had discussed the whole matter calmly and sensibly with Roy. She repented long and bitterly of the things she had said, and knew she had been carried away by jealousy of Claire.

The secret conviction that she had failed Roy in his hour of direst need, and that she had been actuated by jealousy of another woman, by self-seeking love and wounded vanity, grew in Beatrice's heart as the months rolled by.

She knew she had wounded Roy to the quick, and that perhaps he would never forgive her. The memory of her words must be always with him wherever he was. She had broken the most precious thing in her life, and time would not heal the wound.

Beatrice wondered whether Roy still was a cocaine fiend, probably she would never know, and Roy would die out there in the mud of Flanders without her ever knowing how far she had wronged him, or whether she had not wronged him at all. How little it all seemed to matter now before the great issues of life and death!

Whatever his weakness, his folly, his tragedy had been, when the time came Roy had shown he knew how to play the greatest game of all. If he failed to live up to her ideal of him, he would die when his hour struck, as she would wish. And then the thought struck her, and sickened her, that perhaps he was by now inefficient, that the cocaine he had taken, and perhaps was still taking, would ruin him as a soldier; perhaps he was somewhere, in some hospital for nervous wrecks, a misery to himself, and a useless burden to his country.

The only thing of which Beatrice felt sure was that he was not dead; she would have heard of his death.

Claire led her into an old-fashioned café in Regent Street, where they could sit quietly and talk.

"Well, how are you?" asked Claire, as if there was nothing that need be said about a person who looked as well and as happy as she did herself.

Claire was well dressed, in much more expensive and fashionable clothes than she usually affected. Her eye was clear, it sparkled with animation, but it was not the hard glitter of cocaine. Beatrice could see that she had not taken cocaine that day; she could not be sure of anything else. Yet if she had given up cocaine altogether Beatrice would have expected—no, she wouldn't have expected to meet her at all. Claire looked if anything a trifle older, more of a woman and less of a girl. Beatrice murmured some vague reply, and Claire went on.

"No doubt you want to know about Roy?"

"How is he?" asked Beatrice. So much depended on the answer. She felt herself turn pale, and she put hope from her.

Claire beamed. "Oh he's perfectly splendid—he's done wonderfully. Did you hear he had won the M.C.? And he's just been gazetted. He took part in a raid on their trenches, and captured something or other single-handed and blew it up. Only two other men besides Roy came back—he's been wonderfully lucky. He thinks he'll soon get leave. . ."

Claire interrupted herself to order: "Coffee, and strawberries and cream—and have you cabbage lettuce?"

"Yes, madame."

"Cabbage lettuce, and thin bread and butter to begin with, then strawberries and cream. . . raspberries—no, it's too early for them—then coffee and cream."

She turned again to Beatrice.

"I suppose you are up to the eyes in work?"

"Tell me more about Roy."

"Well, it's absurd—I spoil it. Roy writes me such good letters. I can only take the edge off his horror of it all and his state of mind. You must see his letters. Come round some time. I shall be in tomorrow afternoon. Come in to tea. I've been growing all sorts of things in the garden: radishes, lettuces, mustard-and-cress—it all helps the food supply of the country—but you know flowers do better. The London soil is terribly favourable to calceolarias—I don't like them, but they do so well—and London Pride. But I have succeeded with asters and there are one or two Zinias, and lots of Madonna lilies. They suit me, I think, don't you? I think I must cut myself a sheaf of Madonna lilies and go and get my photograph taken in South Kensington by the man who plasters one up in the tube lifts. Do you know all about gardens? I do. Perhaps you don't care for growing things?"

"Oh, yes. Have you been at Chiswick all the time?" Beatrice answered. This was a new mood of Claire's, she reflected.

"Ever since Roy left. I'm all alone. The servants gave notice—all of them—even Jane, who took veronal and wore a wig. They all went at once. I've only got Armance—a French maid—and I sent her away to the Isle of Wight. She isn't at all strong. You must look at her some day. Do you know, Beatrice, I'm sorry now Roy didn't go into the R.A.M.C. I asked him if he couldn't get transferred, but he said not. He says he can't bear surgery."

"Idiot," thought Beatrice to herself. "But why, why, when he can face any horrors for himself?" She had been doing a lot of surgery in the last few months.

"I fancy he didn't want to leave the men, you know, in his company."

Beatrice wanted to ask Claire a question, but it was some time before she put it.

At last, while Claire was greedily mopping up the sugar and cream with her strawberries, she came out with it.

"Are you taking cocaine now, Claire?"

"Now? No, they don't put it in the cream as a preservative, do they? Not more than point two five per cent?" she laughed.

"Do you still take it?"

Claire smiled at her. She was not going to be serious.

"To you, Beatrice, I shall always have to admit that I take drugs. . . Don't you remember you said, 'There's nothing really remarkable about the girl except that she takes drugs'? I could never bear you to think I was quite ordinary."

Beatrice saw that she was beaten and smiled wanly.

"Now I must be off," said Claire. "I'm going to hear Avetis at the Wigmore Hall."

"I'll come tomorrow."

She gave Beatrice her hand and a warm smile, then paying the bill, sailed out into Regent Street.

The following afternoon Beatrice rang, and knocked, and rang again, but no one came to open the door. "Perhaps Claire has gone out and will be back in a few minutes," Beatrice said to herself. It would be silly to have come all the way out to Chiswick for nothing. Perhaps she could get round to the garden; it occurred to her that Claire perhaps was working in the garden and hadn't heard the bell. She tried a small door and found it opened. A moment later she was in the garden. Claire had told the truth—it was lovely—a great row of lilies ran down by the wall, there were roses, sweet Williams, and marigolds in profusion.

What a queer girl, thought Beatrice. But Claire was not in there, and the house door was locked. Beatrice saw that a window was open, and fetching a pair of garden steps she climbed up and got in. She went down to the drawing-room.

It was in a mess, but tidy compared with her memory of it on that dreadful morning. The charred piano had gone and there was a new one in its place. Everything she saw, in fact, would have been perfectly ordinary if someone had not spilt a box of face powder on the hearthrug. That was what had given her the first impression of chaos.

On the table there were several letters from Roy, weighted down with a piece of German shell.

Where was Claire?

Beatrice went all over the house. Everything except Claire's room was in spotless order.

She had certainly given no more parties. In Claire's room the bed had not been made and her clothes were lying about. There was also a loaf of bread and an empty tin of sardines on the chest of drawers. Probably she had had breakfast in bed.

Beatrice went down again, and taking up one of Roy's letters opened it, and began to read it. She felt no scruples. Claire had asked her to come and read them.

. . . B.E.F.

Darling,

Love and the happiness of love can't be put into words. I write like a fool, to tell you of my love which can't be told; I had better have sent you a handkerchief dabbled in my own blood, as one of my mates has just done to his sweetheart, or a wisp of grass tied round with a lock of hair like an African savage. Love letters are only important as fetishes. All they tell one, or can tell one, is: "This comes from my beloved, it has touched the skin of my beloved"; so one puts it to one's mouth quite sensibly, and covers it with kisses. Please don't think that this again is a plea for you to write to me— only ask your new girl Armance to do up your last week's pillowcase or anything, and send it to me instead of to the wash. Do you know out here we are utterly reduced, beyond hope, almost beyond everything? If a London crowd was taken out and made to sit pell-mell all over the network of railway lines outside Clapham Junction, and wait there to be killed by the trains, they would feel the same boredom, and the same fear as we do—but then we can't sleep, can't keep warm, and are so plastered with filth that it's wonder the lice can burrow through it. . . That's the truth about war. Nothing clings to one except the love for the person one is in love with.

"I hate everybody except you only, and dearest, all I care about is that you should be constantly happy. Please, darling, remember always that all that I want is you to be happy. If I could, I would make you always happy; but I can't; so if the thought of me, or my sending letters, or living in that rotten old house, make you for one moment miserable, then please, darling, chuck it all. I mean every word of this. Put my letters into the fire. Lock the house up or leave it open, I don't care, and go away. If you would be happier so, pick up with someone else—only never let anything like shame or pride stand between you and me; so if you want me again, tell me.

"It is absolutely idiotic for you to give one thought to me. You have no duty to me. Arrange your life as you best can, so as to have not one unhappy hour. It is a mathematical certainty I shall be killed before the war is over; all I hope is that I shall die before you do.

"Darling. . . Time and separation alter nothing of my love for you.

Yours,
Roy

Beatrice put the letter down. Her heart felt faint within her. She had not anticipated that Roy's letters should upset her so much. She was deeply shocked by what she had just read. Her fingers trembled as she picked up another one.

Darling,

What an unconscionable time we both take dying! When I got your letter in your hand the world swam. It breathed your presence. I was afraid that, like a wonderful butterfly, it would flicker its wings and be off across No Man's Land. That reminds me. I once found two small children, one of whom had a butterfly, and was holding it in his grimy fist.

"'Ou,' he said, 'I can feel the butter rubbing off.'

"I thought it very tender and pathetic at the time—now I see it is a silly story.

"So you took an overdose again! I don't need such excitements, though I did something nearly as silly myself. I volunteered to fetch one of our officers off the wire. Someone said he had seen him moving. It was only twenty yards from

Fritz, and I felt sure Gordon was dead, or Fritz would have fetched him in himself.

"Fritz is quite decent hereabouts in those sorts of ways. However, as this bloody fool vowed he was alive, I went out and found he was cold and stiff; still, I brought him in, since we were kinsmen, though it was rather horrid. They heard me, and simply sprayed me with machine guns. I lay down with Gordon on top of me, and every now and then a bullet went into one of his legs or arms. However, I got a special extra glass of hot whisky from the Captain when I got in, so, on the whole, it was worth it.

"I think you had better not get off on to anything else, but what you must do is to ration yourself. Get it put up in little lots. It's far, far safer to buy it in little lots as you want it. I know what a nuisance it is for you.

"I beg you don't run any risks you can possibly help; don't run other risks, or if you do, not till you've sworn off that enemy. You see it isn't fair to me. I don't want you to have bigger odds against you than I have here.

"I love only you. I hate everything else, only the poets in the Greek Anthology are exempt, and they are dead and rotten thousands of years ago.

Yours,
Roy

Beatrice put it down. She found she couldn't read any more. The sun was shining, the lilies stood in a straight rank outside. She opened the door and the warm wind blew in. In a state of indecision she picked up another letter and glanced at it.

Claire,

I love you, I love you only. I care for nothing but you, and I think all the people in the world are fools but you. Even out here, where, God knows, their noses have been rubbed hard enough in the dirt, they still bolster themselves up by believing things. Most of the men in my platoon believe in God, and believe in a future life. All of them somewhere believe they won't get killed, and they none of them realise that they will die anyhow, and that there's not much point in living till they go blind and deaf and their teeth drop out. I don't find life sweet. When I have been with you I have been so happy that if we can neither of us live again like that it doesn't much matter when we die. When I hear of your death I shan't wait for a German to shoot me. I shall do it myself at once. All this I know is true, and sometimes all the same I am as weak and cowardly as anyone—and I dream of a good wound that will bring me safe out of it and life with you again.

Good-bye, darling
Roy

The next envelope contained a copy of Roy's Will, with the note: "I write this out, as some fool told me I ought to make a Will."

"I, Roy Gordon, leave all my money to the establishment of a research scholarship to be held at the——————— Institute of Medicine for work on the best treatment of cases of voluntary narcotic poisoning."

"Do you object? Perhaps B. will get it and find a cure, and cure you. Then I shall turn out only to have been missing. That would be a fine ending!"

Beatrice dropped the paper. She could not bear to read more. Roy's grim jest and his Will moved her to tears. She rose and left the house wearily. She felt tired and oppressed by the vast tragedy of the suffering world.

XIII

A year went by, and all that time Beatrice worked with quiet resolution at St. Xavier's. She had been given a permanent post on the staff.

She had written several letters to Roy, but had received no reply. He had determined to break off their friendship, and she saw that he had never forgiven her for what she had said that night in Cornwall. From time to time she heard news of him through mutual friends. She knew that he had been home once for ten days' leave and had spent it with Claire in Cornwall. Brewer had told her as much in the previous September. Then there was a blank. She wrote to Claire, but received no reply. Once Brewer had said to her:

"I met Claire at a party the other night. She's in a most awful state."

Beatrice had not asked him any questions. Inwardly she was surprised that Claire should have lived so long. She rarely went out, and did not encourage her friends to call at the hospital, so that when at the end of June 1916 Brewer was announced and came into her sitting-room, she received him rather coldly. She asked him to sit down, and after a few minutes asked him what he had come for.

"You've no idea where Claire is?" he asked her.

"No—why?"

"I'm trying to find her."

Beatrice waited. She saw there was something more.

"She's not at Chiswick. She's not been there for months. Roy is wounded; he's in hospital, and asked me to find out where she is, and whether she is alive or not."

"I see. Is his wound serious?"

"No—a flesh wound in the leg. Do you know, I think it would rather buck Roy up if you went to see him. You don't mind my saying so, do you?"

"Good Heavens, no."

"He asked after you very affectionately, and he seemed to feel as if he had behaved badly to you. I knew that you didn't correspond with each other. I hope you don't mind my suggesting your going to see him."

"You're a fool, Robert. Give me the address. I'll go tomorrow."

Their first meeting was rather awkward. She found Roy looking frightfully worried and highly-strung, and he seemed to her on the verge of a nervous breakdown. But she knew by some quick intuition that Roy had never been a drug fiend. He had not, she saw, taken to drink or drugs. He might have got drunk occasionally, have taken drugs occasionally; he had never formed a habit which he could not break.

He told her about the offensive on the Somme. He was a Captain, and had recently been awarded the D.S.O. He made no apology for not having written.

"I shall be out of here in a few days, and then I'll come round," he said on parting. Neither of them made any allusion to Claire.

A week later Roy came to see Beatrice directly after he was discharged from the hospital. He had had a Medical Board, and been given a fortnight's leave.

"My wound's nothing," he said, "and they are a bit shorthanded. "We've lost an awful lot of officers lately."

She asked him what he was going to do. He winced, and said nothing.

Next day Brewer came in and told her he had heard that Claire was living with some people—he didn't know where. She had been going about with them—a man and his wife. They were said to be living on her money. It was also said that she had entirely given up drugs, and was very ill. Nothing was known. Roy had apparently vowed to find her, and spent almost all his time wandering about looking out for her in likely spots.

Beatrice knew that there was not much method in his search. He was not employing private detectives, and his pride prevented him from asking the sort of people whom he had known when he was married to Claire.

It began to worry her, and his nervous preoccupation and brooding melancholy seemed to her to be morbid. Roy was not in a normal state of mind. Beatrice had been brought into contact with many cases of breakdown under the strain of fighting. It occurred to her that it was quite likely that as Roy had gone violently to one extreme in his letters, giving Claire complete liberty to do as she liked, professing complete absence of jealousy, he might now have swung round to the opposite pole. Perhaps he was in that state of harassed suffering and jealousy in which many soldiers came back to shoot their wives if they had been unfaithful.

One evening he came in to tea, as his habit was, and stood looking out of the window at the stream of passers-by. Beatrice felt sure that he

DAVID GARNETT

was standing there because he could not bear the thought that Claire might pass there while he was sitting at tea. She reflected that Roy probably did not know why he was looking like this for Claire; he did not yet want to murder her; when he met her, she would quote him his own letters, and Roy would murder her.

Poor Roy, what folly had possessed him to write those letters: now he was reaping his reward.

She went up to him and put her arm on his shoulder, with an infinite tenderness, an infinite compassion. Roy's conscience pricked him, he saw how abominably he had behaved to Beatrice, how in the blindness of his passion for Claire he had hurt her, and was still hurting her. He let her lead him from the window, and sat down in front of the fire.

His handsome face was thoughtful.

"I've been a most awful beast to you, Beatrice. You know one goes almost mad; it's a sort of jealousy that prevents one speaking."

Beatrice, however, had misunderstood him.

"Roy, I've been so worried about you—I can't bear to see you so unhappy, and yet I'm terrified of what will happen if you find Claire."

"What do you mean?"

"I'm so afraid you don't know why you are looking for her, and that when you find her you will do something dreadful that you won't have meant to do, but seeing her will be too much for you. One can't blame people for what they do when they are mad with jealousy. They are in such pain."

Roy looked at her with a grave, troubled face, full of tender kindness. He was reflecting that poor Beatrice had been jealous, and that he had behaved very brutally to her.

"I'm afraid if you find Claire you'll murder her."

Roy shook his head.

"No, Beatrice, you're quite mistaken. What I meant was not that I was jealous of Claire having left me, not that she is living perhaps with some other man, though, of course, that would make me jealous too; what I meant was that I can't share what I feel for Claire with anybody else. I'm jealous of anybody knowing how much I love her. But I see it's absurd, and it's wrong too. It is wrong for me not to be quite open with you and tell you what I'm feeling, because not knowing makes you more unhappy."

"Yes—It does; it does," cried Beatrice. "If I only knew what you are feeling."

"You see I know why Claire has left me; I know why she is hiding from me, and why she has never answered my letters. And even if I were mistaken, and she has really behaved heartlessly, if she turns out to be in love with someone else, even then why should I want to hurt her? There is one thing, and only one thing, I have learnt from killing Germans, and lying out there in the mud. . ."

Roy suddenly stopped, as if he were overcome by shyness, and began poking at the fire.

"But I don't want to preach at you," he said. Beatrice thought she had never seen him looking so handsome or so serious. She could see the ribbons of the M.C. and the D.S.O. on his breast. He was a captain, he had won his way up from the ranks, and he had never told what he had done to distinguish himself.

"Well, what is the lesson you have learnt out there, Roy; tell me?"

"It's not the sort of thing you people like to be told. I mean it's all so silly. Killing people is stupid. One does it because one has to, because one's not quite right in the head. But the one thing I've learnt is forgiveness, only that's the wrong word. Who am I to judge anybody else, and forgive them or not forgive them? As for Claire, I love her, and I couldn't feel vindictive to her whatever she did. Of course, it upsets one, and I'm so dreadfully afraid she isn't happy. In fact, I know she isn't. She always had such silly ideas. She's left me because she thinks she'll ruin me, or because she's frightfully ill, and thinks it will upset me too much to see her. She thinks I shall forget her. She has always felt ashamed of herself for marrying me at all. I know Claire. She's simply living in the gutter somewhere, out of pride." Roy helped himself to a cigarette, and began puffing at it.

"I know she's alive. I found out at the bank."

As he did not speak again for some time, Beatrice said at last:

"Why don't you employ detectives?"

"Well, would you?"

"Yes," said Beatrice, "in your place I certainly should."

"Well, it's outside my code. I suppose I'm limited. After all, she's my wife."

"People do set detectives on their wives, don't they?" said Beatrice, weakly. Roy was probably right.

"I should never do that kind of thing, except by arrangement, if she wanted me to divorce her."

Beatrice sat silent. With Roy she found always that nothing was as simple as she had imagined, and when Roy pointed out his objections or his scruples, she somehow always felt that he was right, and that there were all sorts of things which she didn't see, and that she ought to see.

She had thought Claire was perfectly heartless, that Claire had been unfaithful and was hiding from him, and that Roy would quite likely go and murder her with a revolver. Now it appeared that it was of no great consequence if Claire had been unfaithful, that nothing was simple, that Claire knew his motives and Roy knew Claire's, and that it was all absolutely different from what she had imagined.

"How did you get made a captain?" she asked him.

"God knows," said Roy. "Don't ask me."

Three days later, he went back to France without having seen his wife.

XIV

After that, Beatrice and Roy wrote to each other often. He told her what he was doing out there in that dreadful barren land of wire and death, what he was reading and thinking, and he told her a lot about his men.

But he never mentioned Claire, and Beatrice knew there was another life going on within him, which he did not speak of, and in which she had no part. She knew that he still loved Claire as much as ever.

One day she got a postcard, hastily scrawled over:

> Got a bad one, in my back. Shall wangle St. Xavier's. Look out for me.
>
> Roy

But though Roy had been able to write this in the field dressing-station, it was a long time before he could be brought over to England. Beatrice looked for, and found, his name in "The Times" under "Severely Wounded," and the colour left her cheeks. She knew that if she had been Claire, she would have been allowed to go out to France and see Roy.

Probably Roy would die alone out there in some hospital in France. Beatrice wondered if Claire would go out there. No, it was ridiculous to think of it. Tears came to Beatrice's eyes. She smarted with anger when she thought of how Claire had betrayed Roy's love for her; she felt she would like to punish her for her terrible vice that had wrecked all their lives. She did not reflect that although virtue is not always its own reward, vice is always its own punishment, and that no greater punishment for Claire could have been found than to be the thing she was.

Meanwhile, Roy lay in a hospital in France, hanging between life and death. He had gone out in the open in broad daylight under violent shell fire to save a wounded man. He had picked the man up and carried him back, but when almost in safety a fragment from a shell exploding behind him knocked him over, with a terrible wound in the back.

Roy lay for some time face downwards in the mud, crumpled up on the man he had been carrying, while his blood soaked them both in a tepid, sticky bath. Then he was picked up by a Highlander from his own Company, and carried quickly to the comparative safety of a dug-out.

He recovered consciousness, while he was in the dressing-station, sufficiently to call to a Colonel of the R.A.M.C., whom he saw walking across the room, and ask him for a postcard. The Colonel found him one. When it was written, Roy, turned paler still, and fainted. The Colonel took it out of his hands, and read it. He made a note. If he lived, Roy should go to St. Xavier's. But for weeks it was thought too dangerous to move him from the base hospital. Three operations were performed. At last, three weeks after Beatrice had received the postcard, Roy was admitted to St. Xavier's. Beatrice got a separate room for him, and took him under her especial care.

His life hung on a slender thread. Two ribs were broken, one kidney had been shot out, and a splinter of shell still remained in dangerous proximity to the heart. Beatrice made a long and detailed examination. The most hopeful thing was that Roy had lived so long, but with the shell-splinter where it was, he was in hourly danger. As soon as possible, an operation would have to be performed, and the sharp morsel of metal extracted.

Beatrice made examination after examination under X rays. It was at first sight an almost impossible operation. It was almost inaccessible, yet Beatrice did not despair. She told him how he was in most respects, but she did not tell him the whole truth about the splinter. At first he was incredulous.

"Then, Beatrice—I shall live! How extraordinary! I was certain I had only come home to die. I was positively certain."

"Yes, you'll live all right," answered Beatrice stoutly. And what's more you will be as good as ever you were. Many a fine fellow has only got one kidney."

Roy smiled. What a child Beatrice was; how singlemindedly, how honestly, how finely she lived! How brave she was! Roy forgot his own courage, or rather he had never thought about it. It was natural to him always to be the first to risk his life; he never thought about it, it never seemed to him more remarkable that he should go out under fire to pick up a wounded man, than that he should pick up a hat that had been blown off in the street and return it to its owner.

But in Beatrice's steadfastness, her quiet resolution, her tireless endurance, he saw the kind of courage that he really admired.

Beatrice came to regard that slender dart of steel that lay touching Roy's heart, and that moved with its beating, as a living thing, a force of evil. She felt for it, although she was not imaginative, all, and more than all, she had ever felt for Claire. It was her problem, it was a personal contest, and she felt that she alone could solve it. Several of the greatest surgeons came to look at it, and afterwards in private gave her their opinion on it. With one exception they declared that it was too dangerous to risk an operation, and that it was quite impossible to say how long Roy would live. "He may live for several months, he may last for years, but he'll always have to lie on his back. That those R.A.M.C. people ever dared to send him across the Channel just shows what they are—not that they can help it out there."

There was one great surgeon, perhaps the greatest, Sir Bruce MacGregor, who thought differently. Beatrice had worked under him for years, and she counted for much more than she knew in his eyes. He gazed for nearly half an hour at the piece of metal that lay like a black spearhead touching the grey shadow that was Roy's heart, embedded in the cartilages on the edge of darker vertebrae. Then when he had seen enough, the X-rays were switched off and he went with Beatrice into another room.

"What do you think of it, Miss Chase?" he asked her.

"I think we must operate, though not just yet."

"Nae doubt, nae doubt of it. It is a very serious responsibeelity, but one has to face one's responsibeelities. I would rather see you do it than any other pairson. I have a very high opinion of you as a surgeon."

Sir Bruce MacGregor was all-powerful, and his opinion was sufficient backing for Beatrice to be able to undertake the operation. Meanwhile Roy slowly regained his strength, and the terrible shock which he had suffered wore off. Week after week went by, and he came to feel for Beatrice an awakening of love that was larger, and more impersonal than his love for Claire. As far as possible he avoided thinking of Claire. He felt he was not strong enough.

At last the day came when Beatrice decided that he was sufficiently well to undergo the operation. She had suddenly seen in the middle of the night, by a flash of genius, how it was to be done. She would operate from the front, not from the back. It would involve moving the heart to one side, and it would need an almost extraordinary delicacy and swiftness, but it was, she saw, the only way by which she could draw out the splinter without injury to the spine.

That morning she explained she explained the whole thing to Roy in detail. "It's a hundred to one you'll die," she added grimly.

"My dear Beatrice, I see you're a genius; you've actually saved my life already. In a couple of months I shall be playing cricket again. For goodness' sake believe in yourself, and don't be modest."

Beatrice smiled.

"Now, come here," said Roy. "You've been open with me, and I'll be quite open too. It isn't that I haven't confidence in you; I have. But before you operate will you find Claire, if she's alive. Tell her there is this thing to be done, and that I want to see her."

Beatrice turned and looked out of the window to hide her feelings. She had screwed herself up to operate, but in her concentration on saving Roy's life she had almost forgotten that he had a wife; that there was a stranger closer to him than she was. Claire! Claire was only a name now, a forgotten image. Beatrice had gone so far in the last months, had lived through such ages, that she could hardly believe that there was such a person as Claire. No, there couldn't be, there was nothing but her and Roy and that cruel strip of metal in the world. Roy's words brought her thoughts back.

He was speaking in low tones:

"When I think of my married life it all seems so strange to me now, like something that couldn't possibly have happened to me. If I were to meet Claire for the first time now, I know I could stop her taking drugs. I was a fool, I missed my chance. It will be ever so much more difficult now. I could cure her now—but I suppose I shan't have the chance. You see, I could do it now because I feel quite differently about Claire. I didn't know what I was doing half the time. I was crazy about her. I still love her—but it's a different kind of love. . . and I value life too much to let her ruin it for me or for herself. I had too many fine feelings about Claire, and not enough about anyone else. I'm a lot saner now. I ought to have saved her first and been scrupulous afterwards. But I suppose that if I had been perfectly sane it wouldn't have happened at all. It's all been a delirium since I met Claire, but that's over. What I feel about Claire is what we soldiers keep on saying about the war: if we had known in 1914 what we know now, we should have done things very differently. And if we could start all over again, who knows if we should start it at all? But it's always been a point of honour with me to think I should start again with Claire if I could. . . but since I've been crocked this second time I've felt too weak. God knows I love Claire tenderly. I pity her, but I can't bear to think about her. . ."

Roy stopped speaking, and began to move restlessly in his bed.

Beatrice suddenly felt that she ought not to have let him talk.

"You must not talk any more now," she said; yet what he was saying made her suddenly feel happier than she had ever thought she would feel again. His feelings for Claire had changed.

Roy's face was working painfully; when he spoke there was a tragic note in the weak voice.

"It's awful, thinking of one's mistakes. . ." After a moment he added in a different tone: "Thank God I've made my worst mistakes with my own life, and with yours, not with the lives of my men. That must be awful. If you ask me, generals are the men who never think about their mistakes. If they did they would go mad with shame."

Beatrice knelt beside him and laid her cool hand on Roy's forehead.

"Thank you, Beatrice, thank you; how nice that is," Roy said, and lay still like a tired child, and like a child he took her hand in his and held it tightly. "I love you, you know I love you," he murmured.

Beatrice kept stroking his forehead, and spoke to him in soft, low tones, soothing him as if he were a sick child. All her suppressed passion of love for him showed itself in the tenderness of her voice.

Presently Roy fell into a gentle sleep, and Beatrice released her hand and stole silently out of the room. She sighed when she reflected that she must find Claire. . . But everything was different now. It was all as dreadful as ever, but she could not help feeling happier.

Beatrice sought out Brewer.

"How's Roy?" he asked her.

"I want to find Claire. Don't bother me, but help."

"I saw her come out of a chemist's shop," he told her. I expect they know."

Beatrice called on the chemist. After half an hour the terrified man told her that he expected Claire about dark that evening. He denied serving her with cocaine, yet he begged Beatrice for mercy.

That evening Beatrice waited in a small restaurant on the other side of the street. Presently she saw Claire coming down the street, swinging her arms. Beatrice went out to meet her.

"Claire," she said.

"Hullo," Claire nodded, and passed on.

Beatrice went after her, but Claire spun round and faced her.

"Go to hell! I don't want to talk to you. Can't you see when you're not wanted?"

"I've something to say to you."

Claire's eyes glittered in the lamplight. Her face was hardly recognisable, it was so distorted with sudden passion.

"Leave me alone."

"Roy is badly wounded."

"Leave me alone."

"He sent me to find you."

Claire shrugged her shoulders callously and went into the druggist's shop. Beatrice waited for her outside. After half a minute Claire came out, and with blazing eyes walked straight up to Beatrice.

Claire was very pale—she looked ill. Her lips were bluish, her eyes positively blazed in the dark street. There was something tigerish in her movements and in her anger. She was untameable, more savage in her rage than anything Beatrice had ever seen or dreamed of.

"You've stopped them serving me there, Beatrice." She panted, she snarled with rage horribly, an angry animal noise came from between her bared teeth. For a moment she was at a loss for words.

"I don't care a damn if Roy. . ." She paused. For a moment it seemed as if something prevented her speaking, but after a second Claire went on speaking very fast.

"If you follow me now I'll do for you. If you don't leave me alone I'll do anything. I'll throw vitriol over you, or buy a knife—I'll strangle you. . . Don't dare to follow me." Claire turned and walked away down a side street.

Beatrice had been absolutely taken aback. She felt horror-struck, and at the same time disgusted; she almost turned away and left Claire. She was not used to rows in the street. She waited a minute, then she quickly caught up with her.

"Claire. . . I didn't come to stop your getting cocaine. . . You can take all you want as far as I am concerned, but, Claire. . . Don't you understand that Roy is wounded. He sent me to find you, he wants to see you. If you don't see him now perhaps you'll never be able to see him again."

Claire walked on steadily.

"Claire, don't you remember Roy? He loves you. You used to love him. He is dying. He wants to speak to you."

They walked silently together for a little way. Beatrice was desperate; at last she said in despair:

"I really can't get you cocaine—I mean I won't, but I'll get you an injection of morphine if you must have something, or heroin. That's what we give if we have to give something.

Claire turned half-round.

"Well, get it, damn you."

Beatrice was not used to being spoken to in such a way. Claire's curses were uttered with savage ferocity.

Beatrice led her into a chemist's, and wrote order for morphine. The man looked surprise an examined it carefully.

"I'm an M.D.," said Beatrice.

The chemist asked her to sign a book. When she had done so he led them into an inner room, where Beatrice gave Claire an injection of morphine. They left the shop in silence.

"By Christ, I wish I could make you suffer, Beatrice," said Claire quietly.

Beatrice paid no attention to her remark.

"Now will you come and see Roy? she asked.

"No I won't."

Beatrice led the way to a small coffee-house where they could sit down and talk.

The colour had come back to Claire's lips and cheeks. She looked at Beatrice now with scornful anger and contempt.

"Claire," pleaded Beatrice gently, "Roy loves you, Roy wants you."

Claire's eyes sparkled. She looked at Beatrice straight in the eyes, and there was such an intense hatred in those orbs of glittering blue that Beatrice dropped her own. Claire made a low sound that was half a snarl of contempt and half a sob, the sound that the bravest man cannot keep back in the worst agony. Then she made a gesture as of rage impotent to express itself, of weariness. .When she spoke it was in a low tone hardly above a whisper.

"I don't want to remember. Why do you make me suffer so? Don't I suffer enough without you? Why do you torture me? I don't want to think. . . Oh, I hate you, Beatrice! You think you love him—well then, fuss about with him now he's dying, only don't come near me again. Let me die in peace. Don't tell him you've seen me. Now go, and don't wait for me outside. I've no more to say. If I could hurt you I would. You make me remember things."

They sat for a while silent, then Claire said:

"I shan't live much longer. You—Beatrice—has anybody ever told you, Beatrice, that you're stupid? You're stupid as a horse."

Beatrice had never felt so uncomfortable in her life. Claire got up and went out, and made her way home, leaving Beatrice sitting over the empty cups thinking.

Claire walked bravely. No one spoke to her. She lived in a room over a coach-house in a small mews. She let herself in, and in her room took off her boots and lay down on the bed.

　　　　　　　　　　　　　　　　　　　　DAVID GARNETT

Hours passed, and Claire still lay, sobbing as if her heart would break. She could not stop herself. She was gentle now, she was like a lost child. Oh, oh, oh, she could not bear it! Her sobs grew louder and more violent.

Someone in the room beside her, irritated by the sound, began hammering on the wall with a boot. She was silent.

XV

The next morning was clear and sunny, and Beatrice went in to see Roy after breakfast.

"I saw Claire," she said.

"Won't she come?" Roy asked.

"No. I talked to her for a long time."

"All right. That settles that. I see it was rather low of me to ask her. She would have come long ago if she had wanted to."

Beatrice said nothing. Low of Roy to ask Claire to come and see him!

Presently Roy said to her:

"I expect you want to get this job done. Why don't you do it now?"

"It was all arranged for this morning," said Beatrice.

"Go ahead, then. But come and give me a kiss first if that isn't rather exaggerating the importance of the occasion."

An hour later Beatrice was working quickly on a senseless mass of bone and flesh. Her face was calm. She worked very quickly. Never pausing for a second, she carried the whole operation out in less than a quarter of an hour. Sir Bruce MacGregor sat on one side and another surgeon of world-wide reputation on the other, watching in silence. When it was all over they showered congratulations on her.

"Do you think he will live?" she asked Sir Bruce.

"Nae doubt of it—why should he not?"

Beatrice hurried out of the room to hide her feelings.

That evening she could talk a little to Roy, who had recovered consciousness.

Two days later Beatrice went on with her ordinary work at the hospital. She was cheery with the patients and hearty with everyone. Roy was going to recover. But when she was in the out-patients' ward the nurse who attended to Roy came hurrying in.

"His pulse. . ." she began. "Captain Gordon's pulse. . ."

"Stay here, nurse, and look after these people." Beatrice fled.

It was what she had feared, a bad heart attack. Beatrice did what was necessary in a few seconds. Then she could only sit and watch and feel his pulse. Presently the nurse came back.

"There's rather a bad case I've just admitted. I've put her in the side room. I think you ought to go soon."

DAVID GARNETT

Beatrice nodded. "All right." But she did not move. She felt that she was holding up Roy's vitality; she imagined that if she left him he might die. For ten minutes more she sat there. Then the drug she had injected did its work, and Roy's heart began to beat steadily.

Beatrice got up and tore herself away. In the out-patient ward there were several people waiting to be treated. She attended to them. It was half an hour before she remembered the serious case in the side room.

Beatrice swore under her breath:

"I'm not up to my work. I ought to be shot for that," she said to herself as she hurried in.

On the bed she saw Claire. She recognised her at once.

"Hullo! What's this?" Beatrice spoke aloud, but her words died away queerly.

Claire was lying unconscious. She was silent, she was not breathing. Her heart was not beating.

Beatrice moaned blankly. She seized Claire's arms and worked them up and down in a frenzied effort.

Claire was dead. For a long time Beatrice would not face the fact, but at last she dropped Claire's arms and sat beside her on the bed, holding Claire's head in her arms: Claire was dead.

Tears seemed to come from nowhere to streak her cheeks and blind her, and for some time Beatrice sat sobbing, completely unstrung.

Claire was dead—but Roy, Roy was alive. Roy would be all right.

Beatrice went and found someone who consented to do the out-patients for her. Then she went to her room and lay silent, thinking. Then she went down and looked at Claire. How lovely she was!

Claire lay there in all the dignity and mysterious tranquility of death; her face was in complete repose, calm, restful, happy. She was as lovely and as full of innocence as the day when she had come to meet Beatrice in Cornwall. Now she was dead. What was the meaning of it? Beatrice gazed at her with a strange expression of admiration and respect.

Beatrice had been her enemy; she had fought with her for Roy, and been beaten, but she had known how to live longer. And Claire had loved Roy, in her own way. Claire had been her enemy, hating her at the end, but Beatrice remembered that she had been generous once.

If Claire had not been a drug-fiend she would have been a person whom she could have liked—but Claire's vice had made her impossible. It had made her inhuman, it had entered into everything and spoilt everything. She was an enemy whom Beatrice could respect—she had seen death coming to her and had hurried to meet him, she had gone her way with open eyes. Death! Beatrice spent her life in fighting death, in disputing his advance tenaciously. Mankind were with her; they wanted all of them to live, to have children and live in others. But Claire was a renegade, a traitor: she valued life at nothing

Death—well, Claire was dead now. Beatrice looked at her lovely face, at her childish figure lying there in its mysterious beauty, and then left the room quietly.

She entered Roy's room on tiptoe. He was asleep, and his gentle breathing told her that there was no more to fear. The crisis had passed. A weight slid from Beatrice's heart and she sat down, smiling with girlish dreams and happiness. The future opened out in front of her and limitless possibilities seemed to spread before her. Roy would recover. The war would soon be over, and anyhow he would be discharged from the army. He would, of course, take up medicine again. . . And then. . . and then. . .

Roy opened his eyes and woke up gently.

"Beatrice, is that you, dear."

She sat at his bedside, holding his hands, and for a long while they sat thus, talking gently and looking into each other's eyes in the half-light of the darkened room.

DAVID GARNETT

A Note About the Author

David Garnett (1892–1981) was a British writer. Born in Brighton, East Sussex, Garnett was the son of Edward Garnett, a critic and publisher, and Constance Clara Black, a translator of Russian known for bringing the works of Chekhov and Dostoevsky to an English audience. A pacifist, he spent the years of the First World War as a conscientious objector working on fruit farms along the eastern coast England. As a member of the Bloomsbury Group, he befriended many of the leading artists and intellectuals of his day. After publishing his debut novel, *Dope-Darling* (1918), under a pseudonym, he won the James Tait Black Memorial Prize for *Lady into Fox* (1922), an allegorical fantasy novel. His 1955 novel *Aspects of Love* was adapted into a musical of the same name by Andrew Lloyd Webber. Alongside poet Francis Meynell, Garnett founded the Nonesuch Press, an independent publisher known for its editions of classic novels, poetry collections, and children's books. Garnett, a bisexual man, had relationships with fellow Bloomsbury Group members Francis Birrell and Duncan Grant, and was married twice in his life. Following the death of his first wife Ray, with whom he had two sons, Grant married Angelica Bell, the daughter of Grant and Vanessa Bell, whose sister was renowned novelist Virginia Woolf. Together, the Garnetts raised four daughters, three of whom went on to careers in the arts. Following his divorce from Angelica, Garnett spent the rest of his life in Montcuq, France.

A Note from the Publisher

Spanning many genres, from non-fiction essays to literature classics to children's books and lyric poetry, Mint Edition books showcase the master works of our time in a modern new package. The text is freshly typeset, is clean and easy to read, and features a new note about the author in each volume. Many books also include exclusive new introductory material. Every book boasts a striking new cover, which makes it as appropriate for collecting as it is for gift giving. Mint Edition books are only printed when a reader orders them, so natural resources are not wasted. We're proud that our books are never manufactured in excess and exist only in the exact quantity they need to be read and enjoyed.

Discover more of your favorite classics with Bookfinity™.

- Track your reading with custom book lists.
- Get great book recommendations for your personalized Reader Type.
- Add reviews for your favorite books.
- AND MUCH MORE!

Visit **bookfinity.com** and take the fun Reader Type quiz to get started.

Enjoy our classic and modern companion pairings!